The Treasure of the 'San Philipo'

By *Percy F. Westerman*
(Originally published 1940)

the treasure of the san philipo

Percy F. Westerman

TABLE OF CONTENTS

THE LOG OF THE PRIVATEER "ANNE"
THE WRECK
UNCLE HERBERT'S NARRATIVE
THE CIPHER
A MIDNIGHT ADVENTURE
THE "FORTUNA"
THE EXPEDITION SETS SAIL
A RESCUE AT SEA
AN ADDITION TO THE CREW
YARNS IN THE FIRST WATCH
THE RED SEA
AT THE TREASURE ISLAND
WE FIND THE WRECK
A TERRIBLE ORDEAL
THE DEFENCE OF THE TEMPLE
TOUCH AND GO
WE FIND THE TREASURE
COMMITTED TO THE DEEP
THE CAVE
A GREAT CATASTROPHE
CHECKMATE

Chapter I

THE LOG OF THE PRIVATEER "ANNE"

"REGGIE, my boy, I have a letter from Uncle Herbert."

"What does he say? Has he heard good news about the hidden treasure?

"Yes; but wait till after breakfast and you can read it."

I almost danced with delight at the information, vague as it appeared, for during the last three months news of my uncle's progress in search of the mysterious treasure that was to restore the fortunes of the family had been disappointingly scarce; and, now that there were indications of a flowing tide in our affairs, it was hard to realize that success might be within measurable distance.

My story opens in the year 190—, when I was sixteen years of age, and during the few years that have since elapsed I may truthfully say, without boasting, that few boys have ever experienced a greater amount of peril and adventure than has fallen to my lot in the search for the "San Philipo" treasure.

My name is Reginald Trevena, and I live at Polruan, in a house that has been in the possession of our family for centuries; for the Trevenas are reckoned amongst the oldest stock in all Cornwall. Go back to the time of the Spanish Armada; or the stirring wars of the Great Rebellion, when Cornwall was the scene of many a sanguinary conflict between Cavalier and Roundhead; or the equally exciting period of the Napoleonic Wars; search the contemporary records of those days, and I'll warrant you'll find a Trevena plays a conspicuous and honourable part.

We are of an old seafaring family, and our house contains many mementoes of our ancestors' prowess. For instance, there is the silver-mounted sword presented to my great-grandfather, Jasper Trevena, in recognition of his gallant and successful defence of the Falmouth packet "Restormel Castle" against a French privateer of twice its size; and another relic is the silver-braided cocked hat worn by an ancestor, Humphrey Trevena, at the battle of Vigo Bay in 1702.

It is this Humphrey Trevena who is morally responsible for our search for the "San Philipo" treasure. Briefly, the facts of the case are these. Humphrey was apparently a rough sea-dog who tempered his fierce roving spirit with a peculiar spice of superstition, which, at that period, was rampant in Cornwall. In fact, even at the present day, dread of the supernatural has a strong hold upon the poorer classes of the Duchy, although modern education has done much to banish the firm belief in witchcraft that our forefathers held.

But to return to Humphrey Trevena. From papers in our possession it appears that in 170—, this sturdy sea-captain, who commanded the privateer "Anne," of thirty guns, received orders from Commodore Sir Charles Wager to make an independent cruise, in company with the "Leopard," of twenty-four guns, to intercept a Spanish treasure-ship, the "San Philipo," which was bound from Callao for Cadiz. The Spaniard had a rich cargo, including fifteen chests of pieces-of-eight, twenty sows of silver, and gold plate, the total value being equivalent to £500,000 of our money.

The "San Philipo" arrived at Coquimbo in the month of May of that year, and left on the following June 1. The "Anne" and her consort passed through the Straits of Magellan early in the latter month, but were shortly afterwards overtaken by a furious gale off the Madre de Dios Archipelago, during which the two vessels lost touch with one another. The "Leopard" alone rejoined Sir Charles Wager, and nothing more was seen of the "Anne." Neither did the "San Philipo" reach Cadiz. As far as information could be obtained from the Admiralty, the history of the "Anne" comes to an abrupt termination; but we have in our possession documents which prove conclusively, that Captain Humphrey Trevena did achieve his purpose and intercept the "San Philipo," contrary to popular belief.

The log of the "Anne" is before me as I write; scores of musty pages covered with a crabbed handwriting, made all the more puzzling by reason of the superfluity of flourishes that characterized the literary style of the eighteenth century.

Though too lengthy and too complicated to quote in detail, some portions leave little doubt as to what befell the "San Philipo." For instance, "perceived the Spaniard well-down on our weather-bow. She altered her course and stood N.W., we in hot pursuit." For nearly three weeks this chase continued, during which time the "Anne," in spite of her inferior size and armament, had driven the "San Philipo" into the then practically unknown water of the Pacific.

Although to Cook, some seventy years later, belongs the honour of having made this part of the globe really known to Europeans, there are proofs that the early Spanish voyagers had navigated these waters, the first of them being Juan Gaetano, who, in 1542, made the first voyage of discovery, from New Spain to the coast of Asia. Therefore, I take it, the captain, of the "San Philipo," unable to regain the ports of the west coast of South America, tried to shake off pursuit amongst the numerous coral reefs and islands of the Pacific Ocean.

However, my ancestor goes on to relate how he effected the capture of the "San Philipo" after a stubborn resistance. The "Anne" and her prize made for a lagoon in order to refit; but the reef does not afford the hoped-for protection, for, a gale springing up, the treasure-ship sinks with its precious cargo still on board, while the "Anne," driven south-east by a succession of tempests, is eventually wrecked upon the desolate Chloe Islands, within a few miles of the spot where she first sighted the "San Philipo."

Of the entire crew only Humphrey Trevena and two seamen reach the shore alive, and, after terrible privations, are rescued by a Spanish ship, and kept in captivity, till the Treaty of Utrecht in 1715 caused universal peace.

Now the mystery deepens. My ancestor describes the position, of the wrecked treasure-ship in detail, save that he omits an all-important item. "The island is not more than three leagues in circumference, and is of irregular form. To the south-east is a hill of about 700 feet in height, its outline likened to a cat's head with its ears cocked upright. The outer reef extends roughly a mile from the sandy shore, the opening being visible when two miles from land. The 'San Philipo' lies with her topmasts showing above water (though 'tis certain they be not there now), but fifty fathoms from the western extremity of the entrance, and from it the two headlands on the west side of the island appear in line, and the highest part—*i.e.* that which I have likened to a cat's ear—is directly above the mouth of a vast cave."

This description would doubtless do equally well for a thousand islands in the Pacific; but here the all-important item is missing—the actual latitude and longitude.

That Humphrey Trevena fully intended to make an effort to regain the hidden treasure there can be no possible doubt. Through an excess of caution he prepared an elaborate cipher, giving the exact latitude and longitude, and this he invariably carried about his person in a watertight metal case; but, unfortunately, he met his death through a fall over the cliffs near the Gribben, and when his body was washed ashore the cipher was found on him.

In the natural sequence of events the secret should have come into the possession of his son Gilbert, but, though the latter had the cipher, neither the key nor the log could be found, though search was made high and low, and the secret remained a secret. Vague rumours of the existence of the "San Philipo" treasure floated about, but the majority of Gilbert's friends regarded the whole business as a myth, and the interest in the mystery gradually died out.

The box, with its undecipherable contents, still remained as a sort of heirloom—for, with true Cornish superstition, the bygone members of the Trevena family kept particular guard over the relic of the redoubtable Humphrey—until the year 1850, when my father's uncle, Ross Trevena, having suffered in the general ruin that overtook Falmouth when steamships displaced the famous sailing packets of that port, left Polruan and settled in the neighbourhood of Pernambuco, in Brazil. Here he successfully engaged in coffee-planting, but at length he dropped out of all communication with his relatives in Cornwall, and on his death all trace of Humphrey's cipher were lost, and the faint interest in the "San Philipo" treasure had apparently flickered out.

But, by a pure accident, a new light was shed upon the mystery, and a clue furnished which led to my Uncle Herbert's hurried visit to Pernambuco. Before relating, however, the strange circumstances of the recovery of the log of the "Anne," I must give some particulars of the present actors in this stirring drama.

My father, Howard Trevena, is a typical Cornishman. Tall, broad-shouldered, and possessing an unusual amount of strength, he has a reputation in this part of the Duchy for manliness, good nature, and a love of outdoor recreation, his skill as a yachtsman being well known all along this dangerous coast betwixt the Lizard and Portland Bill.

To me he appeared more in the light of a companion than that of a parent, for, from my earliest recollections, I invariably accompanied him, whether it were, as frequently happened, on a cruise in our ten-ton cutter "Spray." or on a camping tour along the rock-bound coast of North Cornwall, or a cycling tour through other counties of our own country, or even on a ramble afoot amongst the magnificent hills surrounding our home. Although I fully recognize the respect due to my father, I am proud of the complete confidence that exists between us, for he has often expressed the opinion that a parent can make no greater mistake than to treat his sons as children when they are fast verging upon manhood.

My mother died when I was but an infant, so that event, in a measure, accounts for the close companionship between my father and me. And with us, till within a few months ago, lived my Uncle Herbert. He resembled my father in several ways; the swarthy complexion, the close-cut crisp hair, the firm jaw, almost approaching what might be described as "heavy," the steel-blue eyes—all denoted the strain of the Trevenas.

Our house, the ancestral home for centuries past, stands a short distance from the road from Polruan to Lanteglos, on a lofty hill overlooking Fowey Harbour. It is a long rambling building of Cornish granite, with the usual stone roof, the mullioned windows being almost hidden in summer by a wealth of crimson roses. The garden, of considerable extent, terminates at the edge of a steep declivity, the foot of which is washed by the tidal waters of the harbour. In one corner of the garden stood a wooden summer-house, built, so the tale goes, from the timbers of an old Dutch frigate, which was captured and brought into Fowey Harbour during the sanguinary sea-fights of Cromwellian times. In front of this summer-house was erected a white flag-staff; with crosstrees, gaff, topmast, shrouds, and halliards complete, from which flew the burgee and blue ensign of the yacht club to which my father belonged.

You will notice that I used the word "stood" when describing the summer-house, for it was owing to the fact that the structure ceased to be that we came into possession of the log, of the illfated "Anne."

It happened thus: Six months previously, (it was the 5th of November, as a matter of fact) there was a bonfire and fireworks display in our village, and, alarmed by the noise, an enormous black cat took refuge in its terror in our summerhouse. The animal's owner, Mrs. Penibar, a portly old dame, enlisted our services in its recapture, and, armed with lanterns, my father, Uncle Herbert, and I made for its hiding-place.

Right across the summer-house, on a level with the eaves, ran a massive beam, seemingly out of all proportion to the rest of the woodwork, and resting on this beam were several short spars, coils of rope, and other gear belonging to our boat.

Here the cat had taken up its position, and, with arched back and bristling fur, defied all attempts at pacification, spitting and growling in its fright. Neither my father nor my uncle had the inclination to tackle the brute, so the owner, using extraordinary and ridiculous terms of endearment, placed a short ladder, against the beam, and ponderously began the ascent.

Even its mistress's blandishments were futile, for the cat, backing along the beam, still growled defiance. So Mrs. Penibar, mounting to the fourth rung from the top, leaned sideways along the beam and attempted to seize her pet.

Suddenly there was an appalling crash, a shriek, and, amid a shower of dust and plaster, the old lady fell heavily to the ground, and by the feeble glimmer of our lantern we saw that the massive beam had broken as cleanly as if shorn by an axe.

Fortunately there were no bones broken, and, by dint of our united efforts, we managed to extricate the frightened old lady and carry her to her house.

Next morning I arose early and went to examine the debris of the summer-house. Only the walls remained; the beam, deceptive in its apparent solidity, had been hollowed out, and, by natural decay, had gradually become rotten, till the unusual weight of Mrs. Penibar's portly frame had caused it to break, bringing down the roof with it.

All at once my quick eye detected some peculiar object that was half hidden in the heap of rubbish, and, drawing it out, I discovered that it was an old book, bound in rough leather, that was covered in mildew.

Without waiting to examine its contents I hastened back to the house, meeting my father and Uncle Herbert on the threshold as they were about to leave for their usual morning swim—a practice they followed winter and summer alike.

"My word, Reggie! what have you got there?" inquired my father, taking the book out of my hands. For a few moments he looked at its contents in silence, turning over a few musty pages; then, so suddenly that it quite astonished me, he slapped my uncle vigorously on the back, exclaiming, "My word, Herbert, it is the long-lost log of the 'Anne'!"

That day, I remember, the morning swim did not take place, and I was allowed to remain away from the Grammar School at Fowey, and the whole morning was spent in deciphering Humphrey Trevena's faded handwriting, and by night we were in possession of the salient facts concerning the "San Philipo" treasure, though the cipher, giving the latitude and longitude of the island, was alone wanting to complete the information necessary for the recovery.

Good news, like bad, seldom comes alone, and our case was no exception, for next morning my father received a communication asking him to call upon Rook and Pay, a well-known firm of solicitors in Plymouth. On paying the requested visit he learned, to his unbounded astonishment, that his cousin, Ross Trevena's only son, had died childless at Pernambuco, and that a reputable firm of Brazilian lawyers had written to the Plymouth firm, requesting that they should, if possible, find the nearest legal representative of Ross's son.

"We are the sole surviving descendants of old Humphrey Trevena now," I heard my father remark to his brother, on his return from Plymouth, "and, if it is humanly possible, I mean to have a shot at that treasure. Old Rook hinted pretty plainly that there are several heirloom, and the value of the estate, though not abnormal, is worth having. I think the best thing to be done is for you to run over to Pernambuco and get the Brazilian lawyers, Sarmientos, to wind up the estate as quickly as possible. I have little doubt but that you will be able to lay your hands on Humphrey's cipher, for Ross is certain never to have left the metal box out of his possession, and if his son was a chip of the old block, as in all probability is the case, he will have done likewise."

These were the circumstances under which my uncle set out for Brazil, and after an interval of three months, my father informed me, as I have previously mentioned, "Reggie, my boy, I have heard from Uncle Herbert."

Chapter II

THE WRECK

IT was not a long letter that Uncle Herbert wrote; but, on the other hand, it was to the point—

DEAR HOWARD,—

At last I have had this affair settled, and by the time you receive this I hope to be on my way home.

Old Humphrey's cipher, together with several other interesting old documents, is now in my possession, but I am afraid that we are not out of the wood yet, as the cipher requires a lot of puzzling out.

Chappell, an English mining engineer out here, who has done me good service as an interpreter, tells me that all sorts of vague rumours are flying about regarding my presence in Pernambuco, and advises me to take great care both of myself and the papers while I am here. I wonder why?

However, there's no need to write more, as I hope to be back again in dear old Polruan ere long. I've had a draft sent on to the Devon and Cornwall Bank, representing the cash part of the business, as I think it's safer.

Love to Reggie, and remembrances to any friends you run across.

HERBERT.

With Humphrey Trevena's cipher, as well as the long-lost log, in our possession, the outlook certainly seemed more hopeful, and both my father and I looked eagerly forward to my uncle's return. "Just like him, not to say by what boat he's coming," grumbled my father good-naturedly. "I suppose he'll turn up like the proverbial bad ha'penny."

A few days after the receipt of my uncle's letter, I went for a ramble along the cliffs towards Polperro. It was about seven in the evening when I started. All day a thick white mist had hung over the sea, but just before I set out on my walk the mist disappeared with remarkable suddenness, and a strong southerly wind began to send the heavy rollers thundering against the cliffs. As twilight deepened into night, I could see the double half-minute flash of the Eddystone, till a cloudbank obscured the friendly light.

"We're in for a dirty night," I remarked to myself in nautical parlance, and the dark-brown sails of the fishing-boats, showing dimly against the white-crested waves as they ran for shelter, supported my supposition. Before I reached home the storm was at its height, the wind howling over our chimney-pots in spite of the comparatively sheltered position of the house.

"Your Uncle Herbert will be having a lively time of it, if he is anywhere near the Channel," remarked my father, while we were at supper.

"Yes; but it doesn't matter so much on a liner," I replied. "It's the fishing-boats and small coasters that suffer as a rule in these gales."

"That's true; so long as the navigation lights are visible, steamers have little to fear. But, my word! Crosbie was bringing his ten-tonner round from Falmouth to-day. I wonder how he got on. I suppose you didn't notice her in the harbour as you came across?"

"You mean the 'Dorothy'? No, she wasn't on her moorings at five o'clock."

"It's too late to make inquiries at the club," replied my father, consulting his watch. "But I think I'll stroll up to the coastguard station and ask if she has been seen. Put on your oilskins, Reggie, and come too—that is, if you don't mind the rain."

Together we toiled up the steep path that led up to the coastguard look-out hut, and every step towards the hill brought us more exposed to the howling wind and the biting rain, till we were glad to gain the shelter of a rough cairn that served as a wind-screen.

Out of the darkness loomed an object that resolved itself into the coastguard on duty, who, clad in oileys and sou'-wester, kept faithful watch and ward on this exposed and bleak position.

"Good evening, McCallum."

"Good evening, sir; it blows a bit fresh to-night."

"Anything startling?"

"Not so far as I knows of, sir; all the boats 'ave come in."

"That's something to be thankful for," remarked my father. "But has anything been seen or heard of Mr. Crosbie's 'Dorothy'? I believe she is making a passage from Falmouth to-day."

"Mr. Crosbie ain't no mug at the game," replied the man. "Strikes me he's either put back or run into Mevagissey."

"I hope so, too," rejoined my father; and the conversation, which had been conducted by sheer strength of lungs, owing to the howling of the wind, ceased, and we relapsed into complete silence.

From our position we could see both within and without the harbour; and what a contrast! Within the harbour, though the waves caused a nasty "lop," the twinkling lights of Fowey, and the oscillating anchor-lamps of scores of weather-bound vessels in the Pool, caused quite a glare in the dark, rain-laden sky; while seaward, as far as the mirk allowed one to see, was one confused tumble of white-crested waves, which, with a noise that was heard above the singing of the wind, hurled themselves against the rockbound cliffs, sending up columns of white spray, that burst in hissing showers over our shelter, 200 feet above the sea. Not the faintest glimmer of a ship's light was visible, and only the blinking eye of St. Catherine's gave out its warning red flash to break the awful desolation of the raging waves.

"Bitterly cold for May," shouted my father into my ear. "We are doing no good by stopping here."

"Good-night, McCallum," he added, turning towards the coastguardsman; but at that moment a pale blue light flashed upwards in the darkness.

Instantly the look-out man became the personification of alertness. With his night-glass bearing in the direction of the light he waited till the signal was repeated; then, doubling across the open ground between us and the signal-hut, he proceeded to "ring up" the rest of the detachment.

"A vessel in distress!" exclaimed my father; and, following the coastguardsman, we entered the hut to gain further information.

"There's a ship ashore on the Cannis. Message just through from the Gribben. Mevagissey and Polkerris lifeboats called out, and our men to patrol the cliffs between Point Neptune and Pridmouth," reported the man with the abruptness of years of discipline. "If you wants to see anything of the business, sir, our chaps 'll put you across, for 'tain't likely there'll be any watermen about this sort of night."

"We may as well make a night of it, Reggie," remarked my father, "though I am afraid we cannot be of much practical use. Run home as hard as you can, and bring as many biscuits as you can stow in your pockets, and rejoin me at the ferry. We may be hungry before morning."

I did as I was bid, and five minutes later we were crossing the harbour in the stern-sheets of a Service gig, the boat plunging violently in the short, steep seas.

On landing at White House steps (for, owing to the flood tide, it was impossible to make Ready Money Cove), we found that the news of the catastrophe had already spread, and crowds of people were hurrying along the road leading to the Gribben. Staggering against the furious gusts, we crossed the head of the Cove, finding temporary shelter in the wooded slopes of Point Neptune; but, on gaining the high ground at the back of St. Catherine's lighthouse, we were in full view of the sea, only a low fence of wire netting separating the rough path from the edge of the cliffs, against which the waves tumbled a hundred feet below.

It must have been close on two o'clock when we reached the base of the Gribben day-mark, around which were gathered about two hundred persons—fishermen, coastguards, and civilians—all of whom were looking intently seaward towards the Cannis, a half-submerged rock lying a quarter of a mile from shore.

There was nothing to be seen, for the darkness was too intense, while the signals of distress had long since been discontinued—the absence of which gave rise to the most despondent conjectures.

"'Tain't no good waitin' 'ere," grumbled one of the onlookers, a pensioned coastguardsman. "She's broke up hours ago."

"Supposin' some of they chaps comes ashore?"

"What can us do for the likes o' they?" replied the first speaker contemptuously. "Why, with this tide a-makin' to the west'ard, they'll all be corpses long afore they reaches shore. Even if they don't, there's the rocks——" and with a shrug of the shoulders that conveyed a significant meaning, the sentence remained unfinished.

Slowly the day dawned, but the fury of the gale did not abate, although the wind shifted more to the south-west. The old coastguardsman was right: the ship had "broke up," and not a vestige remained.

"What time be 'igh water?" asked one of the men.

"A quarter to five, George," replied another. "See, the lifeboats are off 'ome."

"Do you happen to know the name of the vessel?" asked my father.

"No, sir, we don't; and what's more, we can't make out 'ow she got in there, unless it was she couldn't make out the leadin' lights."

"I think we may as well make for home, Reggie," said my father. "There's nothing to be seen, and no good to be done."

We descended the headland, and reached the sea-level at Pridmouth beach, where the waves were tumbling in heavily, though, owing to the shift of wind, with not so much violence. Under the shelter of a friendly rock, we rested for nearly half an hour, making a sorry meal from the biscuits my father had been thoughtful enough to remind me to bring.

On resuming our way we had just passed the cottages near the grotto, and were about to take the steep path leading to the top of the cliffs on the other side of the little bay, when, a well-known voice shouted—

"Wait a bit, Howard!"

We both turned round, and, to our intense astonishment, within five yards of us stood my Uncle Herbert.

Coatless, hatless, and clad only in a pair of trousers that were much too small for him, a grey shirt, and a pair of canvas shoes, he looked like a regular tramp, while a strip of linen bound round his forehead half concealed his features. Yet it was Uncle Herbert, sure enough, and we stood still in speechless surprise.

"Is that all you have to say to a fellow?" he exclaimed, wringing my father's hand.

"However, in the name of all that's wonderful, did you get here?" asked my father.

"Come ashore from the wreck, of course," he replied, speaking as if it were an everyday occurrence.

"I am afraid you are the only one who did so. Where did you get that rig-out?"

"At yonder cottage. They were awfully kind to me. But let's make for home, for I'm terribly tired, hungry, and knocked about. I'll tell you everything later on."

We began to ascend a steep, tree-fringed path that led up from Pridmouth Bay to the top of the cliffs, and I noticed that my uncle limped painfully. Without speaking a word, my father helped him over the stile, then, one on each side of him, we assisted his halting footsteps.

In this manner we slowly negotiated two fields; and at length came to a hollow, where a rifle-range is situated. Here the cliffs were not more than twenty feet in height, and the sea was sweeping over the exposed pathway. It was now broad daylight, though the sun was hidden by fleeting masses of cloud, and the wind still blew furiously, whistling through the barley and young shoots of corn.

"We shall never be able to get him up this next rise without assistance, Reggie," said my father, glancing at his wellnigh helpless brother. "Just run to the top of the cliff and see if any one is in sight."

Running, while clad in oilskins, is hot and tiring work, and I was almost breathless when I reached the highest part of the cliff path. Not a creature was in sight, so I began to return. Just at that moment, in some bushes to the side of the path, there was a movement, and I caught a momentary glimpse of a face I shall never forget.

A man was lying full length in the gorse. He had evidently been watching us as we descended the hollow. He was without doubt a foreign sailor, judging by his olive complexion, black eyes, long hair, and the large earrings he wore. He was clad in a red shirt, blue trousers, and red stocking cap, while round his waist was a soiled leather belt, from which hung a sheath-knife in a long pig-skin case, and by the saturated state of his clothes and his matted hair I knew he had been in the water. But for an instant he eyed me with a look of diabolical rage on his face, then, springing to his feet, he rushed past and sped towards the town, leaving me standing in bewilderment at the strange apparition.

However, I did not mention the matter when I returned, for it was evident that there were more important things to consider.

"There's no help for it," said my father when I told him of the uselessness of my errand. "We must manage it somehow. Come along, Herbert, old boy," he added encouragingly. "Buck up, and you'll soon be safely home."

My uncle struggled gamely to his feet, and the tedious progress was resumed, but ere we had gone a few steps he suddenly staggered and fell unconscious to the ground.

Thereupon I saw my father perform a feat of strength and endurance which, strong as he was, utterly astonished me. Throwing off his oilskins, he bent down, and, hauling his brother's inanimate form upon his broad back, raised himself and set off at a rapid pace towards Fowey, I struggling in the rear, though I carried nothing but his discarded coat.

Up the steep path he pressed, without pausing a moment; as sure-footed as a goat he trod the narrow way, made additionally dangerous by reason of the slime, and, in less than half an hour, gained the town, never resting till he placed his burden on the steps of the ferry.

Willing hands helped us lift my uncle out of the boat, and, accompanied by a doctor, and followed by a pair of reporters and a knot of curious onlookers, the little procession reached my father's house, my uncle's strange escape from the sea being a subject of much conjecture and not a little romance.

"Absolute quietness is essential," was the doctor's mandate, and in obedient silence our neighbours went away, the reporters following, on hearing that no details were forthcoming, to prepare a column of sensational copy based on the flimsiest material imaginable.

Worn out with my night's vigil, I turned in before noon and slept like a top till the following morning. My father watched by the patient's bedside till nearly midnight, when, satisfied that there was no cause for serious anxiety, and that the expected symptoms of brain fever had not shown themselves, he allowed himself to be persuaded to snatch a few hours' sleep; but before I was awake he was up and about, showing no signs of the physical and mental strain he had undergone.

Uncle Herbert, too, was awake, and beyond complaining of a slight stiffness, refused to admit that he was ill. No mention of the shipwreck had passed between the brothers, but my father, taking me aside, told me that it was surmised that the unfortunate ship was the "Andrea Doria," that being the name painted on a couple of lifebuoys and a shattered whaler that had been washed ashore at Pridmouth Bay, and that my uncle was the only survivor.

"The only survivor?" I repeated. "Then where did that foreign-looking sailor come from?"

"What foreign sailor was that?" inquired my father, and, having told him of my encounter with the mysterious stranger on the cliff, he remarked—

"I wonder what his little game is."

The doctor called again in the afternoon and pronounced his patient out of danger; and, free from the ban of silence, Uncle Herbert began his narrative.

Chapter III

UNCLE HERBERT'S NARRATIVE

"NO doubt you wondered why I returned home by the vessel which came to a bad ending on the Cannis, instead of by the regular mail service. However, before explaining why I took this apparently erratic step, I'll tell you about the documents I obtained from Sarmientos. First and foremost there was the cipher, still preserved in the little metal box. I have not got it here; but, thank goodness, it's safe enough in the keeping of the cottagers at Pridmouth, the same people who kindly lent me the garb in which I made my appearance to you. There's not much in it to look at, but in all probability we shall find it a tough nut to crack. It is a piece of parchment, on which is drawn a square, subdivided into over two hundred smaller squares, most of which are blank, but a few contain various hieroglyphics, and the vague directions, 'steer nor'-east.' However, we will go into that when we get it. The other papers, which, unfortunately, were stolen——"

"Stolen?" exclaimed my father anxiously.

"Yes, stolen; but I was going to say that they were of no apparent value—merely a sort of diary kept by Ross Trevena during his residence in Brazil, the title-deeds of his plantation at San Antonio de Riachaya, a few indentures, and an old piece of parchment, covered with figures—apparently a sort of ready-reckoner.

"As I told you in my last letter, the natives did not appear to appreciate my presence in Pernambuco, or, rather, in the outskirts, for San Antonio is about four miles from the city. Once the *hacienda* where I was staying was broken into, but the intruders were foiled by Chappell's bulldog, Chappell being, by the way, an English engineer with whom I became friendly, and he happened to be staying with me at the time of the attempted burglary.

Twice I was set upon by a party of Brazilians, but the sight of the muzzle of a revolver cooled their ardour, and one night as I was sitting in the patio a pistol bullet whizzed unpleasantly close to my head. Why they bestowed these attentions on me I cannot imagine, unless they had a mistaken idea that I had a secret hoard or a clue to a treasure somewhere in the district. Possibly they do not realize that it is a far cry from Brazil to the Islands of the Pacific.

"However, under the circumstances, I thought that the best thing I could do was to clear out as quickly as possible, and, as it happened, an Italian tramp, the 'Andrea Doria,' was about to sail direct to Fowey to load up with china clay. She wasn't a bad sort of vessel, as foreigners go, being built so lately as 1893, and her captain and officers were quite decent fellows, especially from a social point of view. Probably you remember the 'old man,' Luigi Righi; he's been in this harbour several times, but, poor chap, I'm afraid he won't enter again, unless his corpse is carried in by the tide. The crew were all Italian, excepting a couple of Brazilians shipped to replace some of the men who had deserted at Bahia. Well, we cleared out of the harbour, high in ballast, and had an uneventful run until we sighted the Longships, and here we fell in with thick weather, which ended up with a regular southerly gale.

"We were able to catch only a glimpse of the Lizard lights, then everything was blotted out in the mirk. I stayed up all night, keeping on the bridge with the skipper and the second mate. About 11 p.m. the captain decided we were too close in shore, and telegraphed to the engine-room to slow down to half-speed, intending to keep well out until he could pick up the Eddystone lights, so I came to the conclusion that he thought it safer to make for Plymouth rather than enter Fowey Harbour in such a gale.

"Just as our helm was put hard-a-port, I saw a huge wave bearing down on our starboard bow. It burst over our fo'c'sle in a solid mass, carrying away everything movable, and, hearing a warning shout from the captain, I cowered behind the canvas storm-dodgers, and held on like grim death. The crest of the wave swept the bridge, tearing away the greater part of the rail and the ladder, and with the former went the mate. I could just distinguish his cry of terror above the howling of the gale. The captain slid down one of the bridge stanchions, and, needless to say, I followed suit, and on gaining the shelter of the wheel-house we found that the steam steering-gear had broken down. Almost at the same moment the chief engineer rushed on deck reporting four feet of water in the engine-room, and the quartermaster, staggering along from aft, announced that the loss of the rudder had caused an alarming leak in the after-hold.

"The skipper seemed calm enough, for he translated his subordinate's reports to me; but a few minutes afterwards up came the panic-stricken engine-room staff, gesticulating, and calling on all the saints in the calendar, while from the engine-room-hatch poured a thick cloud of steam, and immediately afterwards the dull throb of the propeller ceased, and we were helpless in the trough of the sea.

"It seemed hours that we drifted in utter helplessness, sea after sea breaking in, carrying away all the boats on the starboard side, while, by the vessel's sluggishness in shaking herself free, I knew she was sinking fast.

"Something prompted me to go below and secure the precious papers, but on gaining my berth I found the cabin door had been forced open and the place hurriedly ransacked, all my personal belongings being scattered on the floor. There were no signs of the documents, though luckily I had the box containing the cipher sewn in my waistbelt. At first thoughts I came to the conclusion that the motion of the vessel had caused the disorder in the cabin, but the sight of the two locked portmanteaux cut open, apparently with a sharp knife, destroyed this theory. In spite of the peril of the situation, I argued that, if robbery had been the motive, the papers, being of no apparent value, would have been overlooked; but further search showed that there was some deliberate reason that had induced the thief to take them.

"In the midst of my hurried search came a shock that made the vessel shudder so violently that I was thrown against the for'ard bulkhead of the cabin. The ship was aground.

"I sprang forward to rush on deck, but, to my horror, I found that the cabin-door had jammed in its frame and I was a prisoner.

"I remember once, when I was a small boy (you were not there at the time), our pet cat was caught by its head in a jug while trying to steal some milk. How I laughed at the wretched creature's antics, as in an agony of fright it tore round the room with the jug adhering firmly to its head. Poor brute! It has my sympathy now, for its state of mind must have been very much like mine when I found myself trapped in the cabin of the sinking ship.

"I was mad with terror. Shouting, I flung myself again and again at the unyielding door, pounding at it with my fists, till, with my knuckles streaming with blood, I was obliged to desist through sheer exhaustion.

Suddenly the doomed vessel listed heavily to port, and I threw myself bodily against the door in a forlorn effort. The framework crashed outwards, and I fell ponderously into the alleyway, where I lay in a half-conscious condition till a rush of water flooding the narrow passage brought back my scattered senses.

"I managed to squeeze through the partially closed companion and gain the deck. The scene of confusion had increased with all the horrors of shipwreck. A few of the less-frenzied members of the crew had lit a tar-barrel, and by the vivid glare of the flames I saw a crowd of half-maddened seamen making a rush for the sole remaining lifeboat.

"In the desperate struggle knives flashed, but whether it was by steel or by water that the wretched, demented creatures met their fate matters little, for directly the boat was lowered it was crushed like an eggshell against the ship's side. There was a short yet terrible shriek of terror, and then the noise of Nature's weapons alone was heard.

"The surviving members of the crew sent up a few rockets, and, in spite of the peril of our situation, we felt cheered by the answering flash from a rocket ashore, and at about the same time the atmosphere cleared somewhat, and I saws a red light giving a double flash at quick intervals.

"Then I knew by the irony of fate that this was St. Catherine's light, and that we were cast on the rocks within sight of home.

"All this time the ship was breaking up fast, and, as wave after wave swept over the doomed vessel, the little knot of survivors grew steadily less, the men being so numbed with continued exposure that they retained no strength to resist their relentless fate.

"I could see that the longer I held on, the more chance there would be of the breaking dawn helping, so that the possibilities of reaching shore in safety would be correspondingly greater, though I had sad misgivings of ever gaining dry land, alive.

"However, I lashed myself securely to a fife-rail, which seemed the least likely to carry away, making a simple hitch, so as to cast myself adrift at the critical moment. The vessel had now listed to such an extent that walking would have been an impossibility, while the remaining portion of the ship trembled under the violent shocks as waves struck the gaping sides and fell in a green cascade over the miserable wretches who cowered to lee'ard.

"At length, after hours of interminable waiting, as it seemed, a grey light began to break over the awful scene, and, looking landwards, I saw the misty outline of the Gribben, though, of course, there were no people visible, neither could they have seen us in that dim light.

"The ship had struck within a hundred yards of the Cannis rock, and in the trough of the breaking seas I could make out the iron standard of the danger beacon, a mockery in our present state.

"At that moment something prompted me to look sideways to see how my fellow-sufferers fared, and to my surprise I made out the figure of one of the Brazilian seamen crawling cautiously towards me. In the semi-darkness I saw that in his right hand he grasped a knife; then, before I could realise the situation, he made a vicious thrust at me with the glittering steel. Even as he did so, the deck seemed to burst upwards, and the miscreant stumbled. The knife fell, but not where it was intended, and, descending on the rope that held me to the rail, it severed it like pack-thread, and the next moment I found myself struggling in the waves.

"I must have been swept across the deck with considerable force, for some time elapsed before I reached the surface, and it was with mingled feelings of despair and exultation that I began to strike out for the shore.

"'Cheer up, Herbert, old man!' I continually exclaimed to myself. 'Everything helps to set you shorewards—wind, waves, and your own efforts. Better be drowned than perish by a knife-thrust, anyway.' And then, in the midst of these encouragements, I thought of the pitiless rocks, and, knowing them as I did, I could form a pretty sure idea of my fate. Just then I noticed something that filled me with renewed hope. The ship was aground, as I have related, within a hundred yards of the Cannis, and now I saw that I was not cast over that jagged rock, but had been borne well to the eastward of it, so that there was a hope—a mere fighting chance—of being swept into the comparatively sheltered waters of Pridmouth Bay.

"I continued to strike out with swift strokes, relying on my strength to last till I reached shore, and my ability to withstand the cold.

"Slowly I neared the shore till the bold headland of the Gribben was abreast, and I had all my work cut out to keep parallel to the ledge of rocks on its eastern side and to prevent myself being swept away from the mouth of the little bay; and, in spite of my efforts, I felt the numbing effects of the icy water gradually telling on my exhausted limbs. How long I kept on swimming I cannot tell, for my actions had become more or less mechanical, till in the trough of an enormous roller I felt my feet touch bottom.

"In another moment I was in the midst of the broken seas, and alternately thrown violently shorewards by one wave and washed back by the undertow, without possessing the strength to save myself, I realized dimly that the little remaining breath I had was being dashed out of my body. Yet in the midst of it all I felt no actual pain, neither did I seem to mind the danger. A vague, unaccountable sensation of indifference gave place to a rapid succession of mental pictures. In a few seconds I had lived my life once again. In times past I have scoffed at similar statements, but now I know it for a fact.

"My last impression of that awful struggle was that I was lying in the soft, yielding sand, with the backwash pouring over me, and the dull roar of an approaching breaker. Then came the crash of the falling cataract, the flash of thousands of brilliant lights, and complete oblivion.

"When I opened my eyes I found myself lying on a rough wooden stool in the garden of a cottage, and a couple of men were chafing my limbs with rough towels. My head throbbed horribly, and I was aware that there was a bandage tied tightly over my temples, from which the blood trickled in a little stream down my face.

"Directly they saw I had come to my senses they carried me over to the cottage, stripping off my wet clothes, and put me into a bed; but, in spite of a dizzy sensation, I soon insisted on getting up, my one desire being to make for home as fast as I could.

"Seeing that I was terribly in earnest, the men rigged me out in some dry clothes, and left me with the intention of borrowing a pony and cart from a neighbouring house; but directly they had gone, a sudden impulse seized me—possibly I was temporarily out of my mind—and I staggered out of the cottage, without reckoning on the long walk home in my tottering condition; but fortunately for me, I had not gone many yards before I saw you and Reggie on ahead, and the rest you know."

"You always were a hare-brained rascal in some respects," remarked my father; "and there was a great possibility of your pegging out through sheer exhaustion, in which case there would have been no survivors from the ill-fated 'Andrea Doria.'"

"Then I suppose I am the only survivor?" asked my uncle.

"I have every reason to believe so," replied my father sadly.

"I think not—at least, I believe I'm right," I exclaimed. "But I didn't like to interrupt Uncle Herbert at the time." And thereupon I told him about my meeting with the foreign-looking sailor on the cliff.

"Yes, I remember you mentioned the circumstance to me," remarked my father. "But why do you suppose the man was a member of the crew of the 'Andrea Doria'? Foreign sailors are not unusual in Fowey."

"But foreigners in saturated clothes do not generally lie concealed in long grass early in the morning."

"What was he like?" asked Uncle Herbert anxiously.

"That's the man to a certainty," declared my uncle decisively, when I had completed the description. "Paulo, they called him. He was one of the two Brazilians we had aboard, and he it was who tried to stab me with a knife."

"Why?"

"That's where you have me. I cannot even guess—unless he was after the cipher."

"Then possibly it was he who stole the papers from your cabin?"

"More than likely. Mark my words, Howard, there is some villainy afoot. Don't you think it would be advisable to set the police on his track?"

"Pooh!" exclaimed my father contemptuously. "We'll hear or see no more of him. Even now he may be working his passage homewards. However, that reminds me: I'll go over to Pridmouth to-morrow and return those well-fitting clothes you were rigged out in, and, at the same time, I'll get hold of the cipher; for, really, I am burning with impatience to tackle the mystery."

Chapter IV

THE CIPHER

SOMEHOW, or the other the news of my uncle's adventures were noised abroad far beyond the limits of our village, and for a week or more we were besieged with letters and telegrams from various people, most of them absolute strangers, offering congratulations, but more frequently asking impertinent questions about the "San Philipo" treasure. Several London and county papers sent representatives down to interview the survivor of the wreck; but to all requests my uncle turned a deaf ear, politely yet firmly refusing to give any information, so that interest in the mystery grew rather than waned; and exaggerated rumours, amusing no doubt to others, appeared in various journals, greatly to my father's and uncle's disgust.

In accordance with his resolution, my father went over to Pridmouth and obtained the metal box with its precious contents, together with the clothes my uncle was wearing at the time of the shipwreck. Curiously enough, his watch, which had been in the water for nearly an hour, was practically uninjured, only a faint trace of rust showing near the hinge, while, on being rewound, it ticked as merrily as ever.

We had arranged to defer the opening of the box till the afternoon, when all three of us would be present; but I firmly believe my father could not resist the temptation of glancing inside to make sure the parchment was still there.

He arrived home in high good humour, for on the return journey, he had picked up a horseshoe and had crossed the ferry in company with a hunchback, both of which incidents are regarded, even in these matter-of-fact days, as being conducive to a run of "good luck"; and preparations were immediately made for the examination of the mysterious relic of old Humphrey Trevena's seafaring days.

I handled the box with a feeling almost of reverence. It was about the size of a cigar-case, and made of a dull, heavy metal resembling bronze, although tarnished with the effects of time and exposure to the salt water. It was embellished on the front of the outside by quaint figures representing Boreal urging a seventeenth-century frigate on its course, with Neptune and Britannia holding a friendly conference in the background, and, on the back, by a monogram of letters "H.T." and the date 1719.

"Open it, Reggie," said my father; and, after I had fumbled about with the spring for a few moments, the lid flew open, and I saw for the first time the puzzling piece of parchment which was fated to lead us through great perils by land and by water ere we accomplished our quest.

With trembling hands I unfolded the paper, my father and uncle looking eagerly over my shoulder. As Uncle Herbert had already informed us, there was nothing but a big square subdivided into a host of smaller ones, and a few unintelligible words and the symbols of degrees, minutes, and seconds of latitude and longitude, with no figures given, save a solitary figure 1.

Here, in fact, is a copy of it—

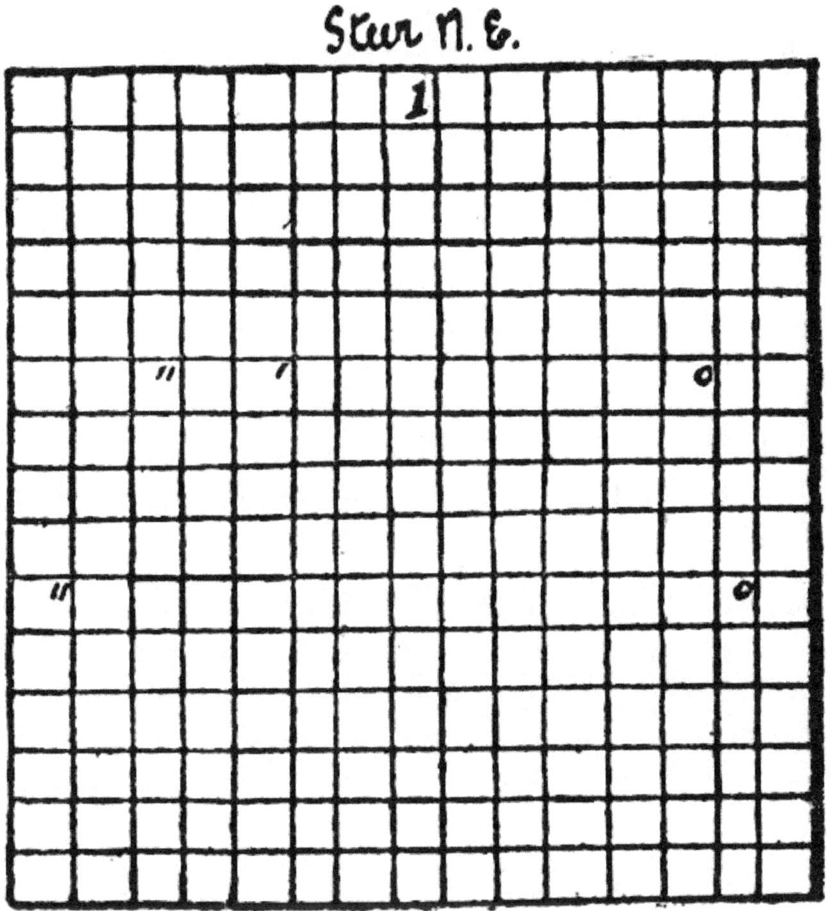

"Well?" asked my uncle, elevating his eyebrows. "What do you make of it, Howard?"

"Give me time. What does he mean by 'steer nor.'-east,' I wonder?"

"That's what has been puzzling me, for in his log Humphrey states definitely that he followed the 'San Philipo' in a nor'-westerly direction, consequently the directions appear to be misleading."

"Possibly they were intended to be so," replied my father dryly. "But these marks of latitude and longitude—do they convey anything?"

"Nothing, except that certain numbers are evidently intended to fill in the squares so indicated, and the puzzle is, what are these numbers?"

"Ah, what?"

"I tell you what; I can see it all now. Amongst the other papers that were stolen was the key to the cipher. Don't you remember my saying that one sheet contained a host of figures? Howard, old man, I am a careless idiot and deserve to be kicked for my negligence."

"It can't be helped," replied my father philosophically. "What is done cannot be undone, so the less said about it the better. We must rack our brains to find a solution to the cipher without the aid of the key. Don't look so glum, Herbert. Better luck next time."

Long after I had gone to bed my parent and his brother pored over the stubborn cipher, either with the aid of frequent references to the log of the "Anne" or the chart of the Pacific, which had been ordered from Potter's some time ago. They must have sat up half the night, for they were both late at breakfast next morning and were horribly short-tempered in consequence.

I went to school that morning as usual, but the excitement of the previous day proved too much for my attention, and, in consequence, I was sent to detention for an hour. If there is anything I loathe, detention holds an easy first, for the monotony of an hour's imprisonment at the end of the day, is particularly galling to a boy fond of outdoor pursuits. I am sure the junior masters do not appreciate the task of looking after the delinquents either, and Newman, the Second Form master, was no exception. So in less than a quarter of an hour he cleared out, leaving us to our own devices.

The fellow at the desk next to mine, a boarder named Ward, of the Upper Fifth, who was ever in hot water, was busily engaged in covering sheets of paper with roughly drawn lines, and as he appeared to derive a considerable amount of satisfaction from the task, I remarked:

"What are you up to, Ward; noughts and crosses?"

"Noughts and crosses, my grandmother!"

"What, then?"

"Trying my hand at a magic square."

"A magic what?"

"Square, you ass! look and see for yourself."

On closer examination I found that he had drawn a rough square and had subdivided it into nine smaller ones, by means of two horizontal and two vertical parallel lines, and the spaces thus formed he was busily filling in with the numbers 1 to 9.

"What happens when you finish it? Where does the magic part of the show come in?" I asked. "It seems a very tame sort of amusement."

"Not when you get thoroughly interested in it," replied Ward. "You see, the idea is to arrange the figures so that each of the horizontal, vertical, and diagonal rows make a total of fifteen. It takes a bit of juggling, I assure you, and I am told that even larger magic squares can be formed. Ah! That's done it."

With a slightly growing interest I watched Ward manipulate the figures until he arrived at the solution, which, for some unexplained reason, I copied down—

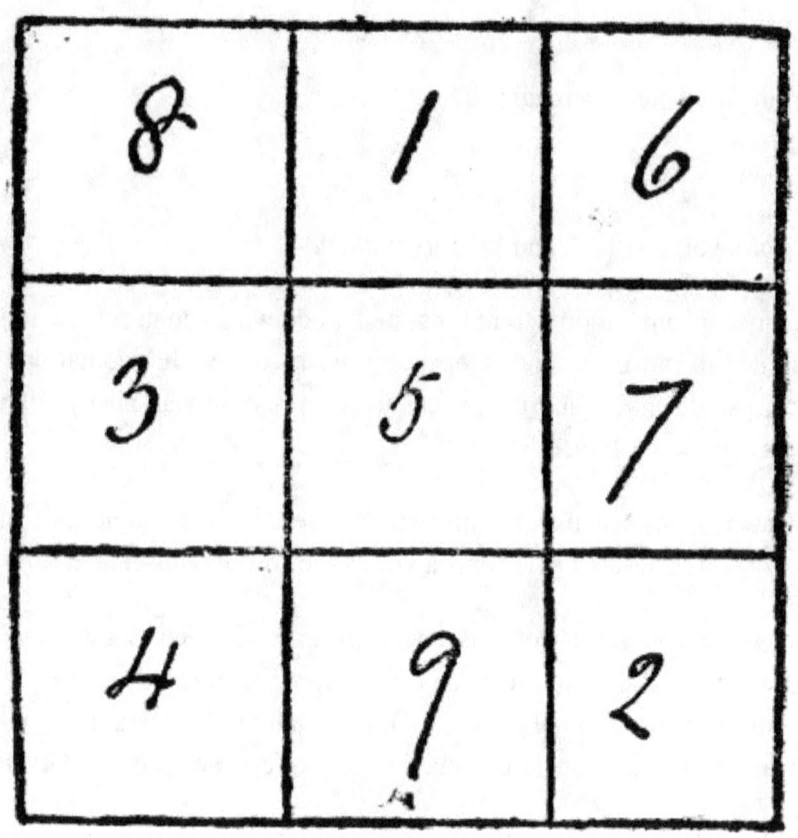

"There are other arrangements of the numbers," he remarked; "for instance, you can get another magic square by exchanging the top and bottom lines or the outside vertical columns; but I have not managed a larger square yet. Hello! Here comes Newman, so it must be close on half-past five."

The miserable hour over, I made my way homewards, revolving in my mind the problem of Humphrey Trevena's cipher, till by some unaccountable impulse, as I was sitting in the ferry-boat that plies between Fowey and Polruan, I formed some hazy connection between Ward's magic square and the exaggerated chessboard design that was so sorely puzzling my father and uncle.

Rapidly the connection grew, till by the time the boat ran alongside Polruan quay-steps I firmly assured myself that Old Humphrey's cipher was based on the principle of a magic square; and, arguing that the solution of the "fifteen" square must be governed by some fixed rule, I determined to try to solve the working of Ward's puzzle, and to apply the principle, if possible, to the more complicated cipher.

With this object in view, I began my task. My father and uncle had gone out to the Yacht Club, so that I knew I should be free from interruption.

My first step was to make a copy of the magic square and indicate the order of the numbers by straight lines from one to the other. When completed, the diagram looked positively bewildering, and the only information I could gather was that the numbers 4, 5, 6 formed one of the diagonals, and ran obliquely from the bottom left-hand corner to the upper right-hand one, and that the centre number was the 5, or, the numeral next to half the highest number of the squares.

Next I tried a "twenty-five" square, the diagonal reading 11, 12, 13, 14, 15. The position of the 1 I had already fixed by that in the smaller square, which, by a sudden inspiration, I remembered occupied the same relative position in Humphrey Trevena's cipher. As in the "nine" square the 7 came immediately below the 6; I adapted the principle by placing the 16 in the square below the 15.

All this took time, but I felt satisfied that I was on the right track, till I came to the rest of the numbers, and, try how I would, I could not apply the principle any farther.

At length, with bewildered brain and aching head, I gave up the task for the time being, and, putting on my cap and calling my dog, I set out for a ramble to try and cool my heated brow.

I intended to walk in the direction of Lanteglos, and make a circuit through Hall Walk, Bodinneck Ferry, and Fowey, but, on reaching the little hamlet of Pont, I sat down on the handrail of the little wooden bridge, and amused myself by sending the dog into the water. At length I desisted, and, ignoring the antics of my faithful companion, I fell into a brown study—a thing under ordinary circumstances I rarely do.

Twilight was drawing in, and against the vivid red hue in the western sky the placid waters of the tree-fringed creek made an entrancing picture, that harmonized with my dreams of adventure in the future, like a presage of good fortune.

Unconsciously I found myself toying with a pocket compass I invariably carried, and as my eyes lingered for a moment on the delicately balanced needle, I saw in my mind's eye, not the compass card, but the outlines of a magic square, with the needle forming the puzzling diagonal. In the haphazard position I held the compass the needle pointed to N.E. on the card, and, like a flash, occurred the directions scrawled upon the mysterious cipher, "Steer nor'-east."

"I have it!" I exclaimed aloud in my excitement. "'Steer nor.'-east' must be old Humphrey's way of expressing the sequence of the numbers on his cipher; and that is the direction of the diagonal."

Without a moment's delay, I hastened home to make a fresh onslaught upon the puzzle, and, to make a long story short, I solved the "twenty-five" square by constructing two similar squares on its north and south sides— i.e. the top right-hand sides—and starting with the figure 1 and working in a N.E. direction, so that directly a number fell within one of the divisions of the adjacent squares, I transferred it to the corresponding division of the original design. But when by this means I came to a space already occupied by a number, I found, by consulting the already completed nine-divisioned square, that the next number was placed in the vacant space that invariably occurred below.

The completed square, which I regarded with considerable satisfaction, appeared as under—

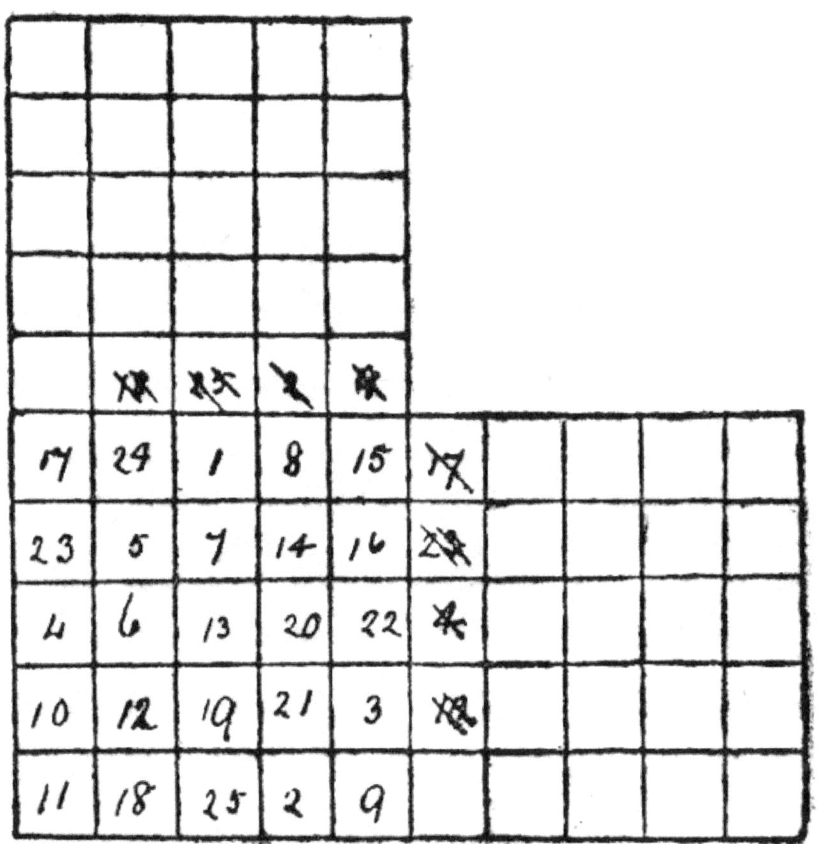

Total of each vertical, horizontal, and diagonal line = 65.

Total of each vertical, horizontal, and diagonal line = 65.

Now came the crucial test of constructing a square with the same number of subdivisions as there were on Humphrey's cipher, and an intelligent application of the figures to the symbols of latitude and longitude; but here

I was nonplussed, for I had no copy of the cipher, neither could I remember the actual numbers of subdivisions.

Just then, however, my father and uncle returned, and while at supper they did not fail to notice my excitement.

"Whatever is the matter with you, Reggie?" asked Uncle Herbert. "You look like a cat on hot bricks."

I was burning with impatience to let them know of my evening's work and its results, but, fearing that after all there might be some flaw in my theory, and having another motive in view, I managed to restrain myself.

Little more was said during the meal, but on its completion preparations were made to continue the investigations of the mystery.

"I say, pater," I exclaimed. "Don't you think it would be better to make a copy of the cipher: it would save the original, you know."

"Just so, Reggie, I will; but I think it's about time you went to bed."

"Another hour won't make much difference," I replied. "You see, to-morrow's a holiday."

My father assented, and gleefully I set about the task of making a duplicate of the cipher, of which I was now firmly convinced I held the key.

It was not a long business, and when completed, I stealthily removed a second copy which I had obtained by means of a carbon paper, and announced my intention of "turning in."

It was, however, far from my thoughts to go to bed, and directly I reached the solitude of my room I set to work to fill up the blank spaces of the cipher, which, thanks to my previous trials with the smaller squares, was a comparatively rapid and easy task.

Total of every horizontal, vertical row = 1695

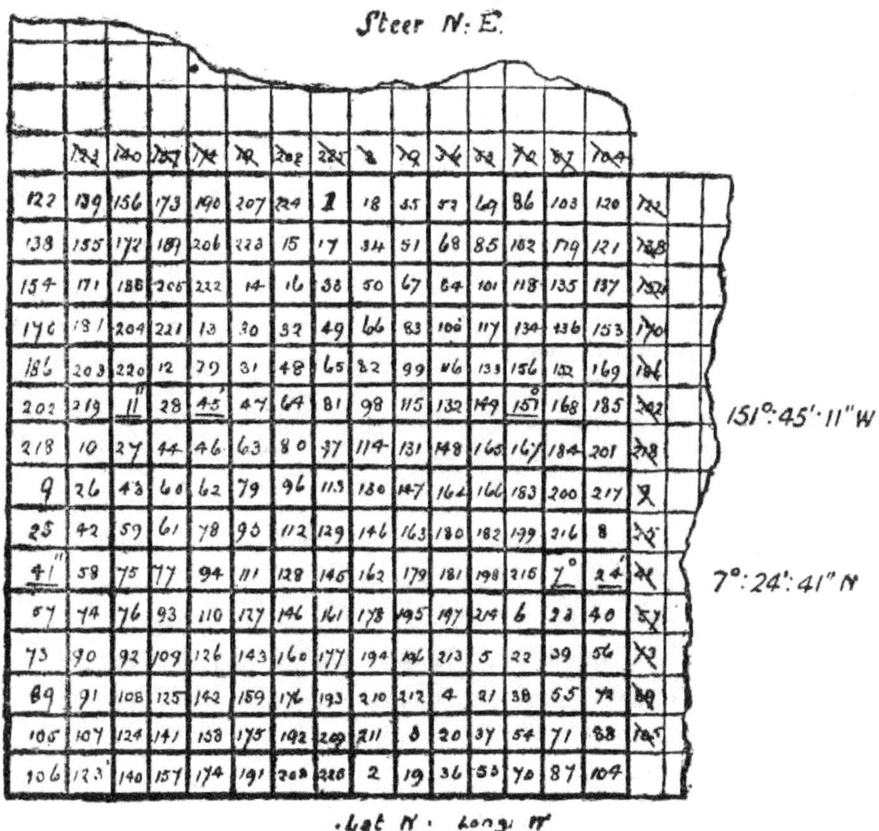

Total of every horizontal, vertical, and diagonal line = 1695

THE SOLVED CIPHER.

In less than an hour I had completed the solution, checking the totals, which in every case amounted to the sum of 1,695; and, applying the marks of latitude and longitude, I found that the position was 7° 24' 41" N. and 151° 45' 11" W., which, in spite of the absence of an atlas, I knew would be somewhere in the Pacific Ocean.

Cautiously I made my way downstairs, holding the completed cipher rolled tightly in my hand. The dining-room door was slightly ajar, and through the opening I could see my father and uncle leaning over the table, which was littered with charts, papers, and writing materials.

"I am afraid we are checkmated," I heard my father remark despondently. "The treasure of the 'San Philipo,' will never come within our grasp."

As I entered the room they both looked up in amazement.

"Reggie!" exclaimed my father deprecatingly.

"All right, pater," I replied, with the boldness acquired by my success. "I want to make a bargain with you."

"A bargain? I don't understand."

"What I mean to say is this: If you make a search for the 'San Philipo' treasure, promise me that I can go too."

"Bless the boy!" ejaculated Uncle Herbert. "What does he mean?"

"The possibility of a search is very remote," said my father, "as we have absolutely no definite information to work upon, and no likelihood of gaining any; but I really don't understand what you mean by the word 'bargain.'"

"I mean," I replied stoutly, "that if I find a key to the cipher, do I take part in the search?"

"I see no reason why you shouldn't if——"

"Then you promise?"

"Yes."

"Thanks," I replied, flourishing the paper I held in my hand.

Chapter V

A MIDNIGHT ADVENTURE

"EXPLAIN yourself, you young rascal," exclaimed my uncle, gripping me by the shoulder in his excitement.

In reply I handed over my solution, explaining in a few words the principle of the magic square. For a few moments neither of them spoke. The pater, seizing a ruler, made a rough pencil mark on a chart of the Pacific that lay on the table; then, bringing his powerful fist down so heavily that the glasses and drawing instruments fairly jumped, he almost shouted—

"Why, you are a regular brick, Reggie! That's it right enough."

"Are there any islands shown on the chart?" asked my Uncle Herbert.

"Several; but let's turn up Findlay's Directory of the Pacific. Hello! What have we here? 'Truk or Hogoleu Islands. This group is composed of four or five lofty basaltic islands, surrounded by a barrier reef.... Discovered by Captain Duperrey, June 24, 1824' (that is, if Humphrey Trevena hadn't done so a century before). 'The northernmost of the group is in lat. 7° 42' 30" N.' (probably San Philipo Island skipped the navigator's memory). It seems possible that an island does exist at this position eh, Herbert?"

"Certainly. Do they give any further information?"

"Yes; here is a choice piece: 'Captain Cheyne, of the brigs "Naiad" and "Will-o'-the Wisp," came here to collect bêche-de-mer, and were completely taken off their guard by the apparent friendliness of the natives, who at first assisted them to build their curing-houses. As soon as the "Naiad" left, they attacked the "Wisp" with a force of 2,000 men, and were only repulsed with desperate fighting and the loss of six killed and five wounded. They also seized the long-boat, which was recovered the same day.... They had a great number of large Spanish knives, and were armed with brass-hilted cutlasses.'"

"'Spanish knives and brass-hilted cutlasses,'" repeated my uncle. "That's strange."

"It certainly points to a wreck of some Spanish war-vessel in bygone days."

"What do you intend to do in the matter?"

"Why, fit out an expedition," replied my father decisively. "I've already formed a rough plan of action, but it is too late to discuss it to-night. It's time we were all turned in and fast asleep."

So saying, my father swept the papers and charts off the table, locked the former in a safe, and placed the metal box with the now solved cipher in his pocket, then motioned us to retire, and extinguished the lamp.

But for me, sleep was an impossibility. The exciting events of the past few days, culminating in my fortunate discovery, kept me awake, and in almost a fever of suppressed mental activity I was continually turning from side to side in a fruitless endeavour to sleep.

Outside the wind was howling across the harbour, making the trees shiver and creak in a weird and disturbing manner. Presently the clock struck two, and at almost the same time a current of air rushed into my room, causing the half-open door to swing back against the wall.

"Surely they cannot have forgotten to shut the hall door," I thought, and, jumping out of bed, I walked silently towards the staircase. The other inmates had been more fortunate than I; my father was sleeping soundly, while his brother was snoring heavily, the place seemingly trembling under the vibrations of his sonorous efforts, and even as I listened I heard a faint click as if the dining-room door was being opened.

Instantly I crept into uncle's room, gently closed the door, and shook him by the shoulder.

"Wake up!" I whispered. "There's some one broken into the house."

"No luck," he muttered. "Twenty fathoms down. Try again to-morrow," and, turning over, he recommenced his discordant snoring. "Wake up!" I repeated, redoubling the shaking performance. "There's a burglar after the cipher."

The word "cipher" did it, for in an instant he was up and fully awake.

"Hush! Listen!" And carefully opening the door, I hastened to my father's room to arouse him.

We sallied forth to meet the foe; my father and uncle led the way, the latter grasping a revolver, while I followed, feeling somewhat disjointed in my lower limbs.

At the top of the stairs we waited for further signs of the burglar, and in the dismal silence, broken only by the moaning of the wind, I could feel my heart throbbing violently against my ribs. At length came the unmistakable sounds of some one moving cautiously.

A man must naturally feel at a disadvantage when, clad mainly in pyjamas, he is forced single-handed to tackle a house-breaking ruffian; but, with three of us, and the comforting reassurance imparted by the revolver, the deficiency of wardrobe counted for little.

Suddenly the silence was broken by the noise of a furious scuffle, followed by a shriek of pain, and, concealment being no longer necessary, the brothers dashed downstairs. My uncle led in the race, but, tripping over a man's body, he lay half-stunned, while my father, who followed more cautiously, narrowly escaped the same fate. Then some one rushed quickly through the hall and began to fumble with the lock of the front door, and, as the door was thrown violently open, there was a blinding flash from the vicinity of the floor, followed by another yell of pain, and the pungent smell of gunpowder filled the air.

"That's settled his hash, Howard," I heard my uncle exclaim. "Get a light and see what we are up to."

I made for the dining-room to light the lamp, and as I crossed the hall my bare feet stepped in a pool of warm liquid. With trembling fingers I struck a match and lighted the lamp, and, returned to the scene of the struggle.

My uncle was leaning against the wall, the still smoking revolver in his hand, and my father was leaning over a motionless figure huddled at the foot of the stairs, while a stream of blood, through which I had stepped, slowly welled across the floor.

"The man has been stabbed!" exclaimed Uncle Herbert. "Whatever does it mean?"

"Get another light—a hurricane lamp, there's one in the kitchen—and run the other man down. You winged him right enough, Herbert; he can't be far away."

The light was procured, and following a well-defined trail outside the door, we ran the other burglar to earth, in a shrubbery close to the garden gate.

Simultaneously, my uncle and I recognised him—it was the Brazilian seaman who had tried to stab my uncle on the wreck, and whom I had seen lying on the cliff path.

While my uncle covered him with a revolver, for he snarled viciously like a wounded animal at bay, my father relieved him of his knife, and, lifting him by their combined efforts, they carried him into the house; but before reaching the door he had fainted.

"He's shot through the fleshy part of his right leg," said my father. "Just put on a temporary bandage till we can attend to the other beauty. Whatever made them fight each other like that, I wonder?"

"I don't know," replied my uncle, ripping the man's trousers with a penknife and winding a long strip of linen round the wound, for the bullet had cut a clean hole right through the Brazilian's leg. "But you see there is something very mysterious in the manner in which this scoundrel has followed me up."

"Now for the other man," exclaimed my father. "I am afraid he has been badly hurt. Why, Herbert, you have had a gash yourself—look!"

"Pooh! A mere nothing. I hardly felt it."

"But it's bleeding pretty freely."

"Yes, the Brazilian made a jab at me as he broke away. But who's this?"

They had lifted the man who had been left lying at the foot of the stairs, and carried him, still unconscious, into the kitchen. He was apparently quite a young man, with closely cropped hair and clean-shaven face, or, rather, his chin was covered with a four days' growth of bristling hair, while his dress consisted of a close-fitting suit of dark blue cloth, the coat-tails tucked in under the trouser band. "Here's a fine bird!" remarked Uncle Herbert, as he began to cut away the odd-looking clothing to get at a wound in the man's side. "You know where he comes from?"

"No," replied my father.

"Bodmin. He's escaped from the naval prison."

"I wonder what he's been up to," remarked my father thoughtfully. "A naval prisoner does not usually associate with foreign seamen, and burglars to boot."

"It's a clean cut, and not particularly dangerous," announced Uncle Herbert. "Bring the light closer, Reggie. Hello!" he added, looking at my face, which must have been horribly white. "This won't do. Run away to the other room, and, keep your head between your knees till you feel better. I can't have three patients on my hands."

I did as I was bid, for everything was beginning to whirl round. Presently my father came in to get some brandy, for the second patient was recovering. As daylight began to dawn, they carried the man upstairs to my room, and presently, after a good deal of talking, my father and uncle came downstairs.

"Run upstairs and get your things on, Reggie," said my father. "I want you to fetch the police sergeant. But, remember, don't say a word to any one about the man we have upstairs. It's only the Brazilian we are going to give in charge; he's coming to now. Remember what I say, and I'll tell you the reason later."

"Did I understand him to say that the Brazilian was coming downstairs?" I heard my father remark.

"Yes, I believe so," replied my uncle.

"Then he must have been in one of our rooms. Only to think that that dirty scoundrel was hanging around us with his knife while we were asleep! I'll go upstairs and see if anything is touched."

A moment later I heard my father shout, "It's gone!"

"What's gone?" asked Uncle Herbert.

"The box containing the cipher."

"It can't be far, at all events," said my uncle. "Let's search the brute."

I am afraid they were none too gentle with the man, but a thorough search revealed nothing.

"Try the place where we caught him," suggested the pater, and we all three went outdoors, carefully examining the well-defined trail. After a lengthy search we found, not only the box, but a bundle of papers cunningly hidden under the shrubbery in a tangled mass of twigs and leaves.

After glancing at the contents of the metal box, which was still intact, my father opened the packet of papers, and, to our surprise, they were the actual documents filched from my uncle's cabin on the ill-fated "Andrea Doria."

"You have only forestalled Fate by a few hours, Reggie," remarked the pater. "You see, here is the exact key to the cipher—the figures your uncle took to be merely business papers. However, run on down for the police."

As I passed through the hall to get my cap, I gave an involuntary exclamation of surprise, for there were no signs of the Brazilian.

In reply to my shout, my father and uncle came running up, and their astonishment was, in spite of the situation, comical to behold. We made a hasty yet thorough search of the house and grounds, with no result. The man had vanished as completely as if he had been provided with wings.

"But he cannot get far, with a badly wounded leg," I remarked.

"It certainly is strange; but he must have a wonderful nerve to play 'possum like that. However, I think we need not send for the police, after all; for they will think we are either mad or else inventing fairy-tales."

Everything considered, there was not much to grumble about. We had, it is true, a wounded man on our hands, and Uncle Herbert had received a slight cut from the Brazilian's knife; but as a set-off we had regained the papers, though they served merely to confirm my solution to the cipher, while the Brazilian, who had an ounce of lead through his leg, would hardly care to repeat his burgling exploits after such a disastrous ending to his first attempt.

While at breakfast they told me about the wounded man upstairs, and why I was not to have mentioned him to the police.

The man, who gave his name as Alec Johnston, a Scotsman, had broken out of Bodmin Naval Prison, where he had been sent after being sentenced by court-martial for the heinous offence, in naval law, of striking a superior officer. He appeared, said my father, to be a well-set-up, healthy young fellow, with a fair amount of intellect, and there was no reason to doubt his story.

Left an orphan at an early age, he was sent by his relatives to the training-ship "St. Vincent." In due course he was "passed out" and sent on a sea-going ship, and, by thorough devotion to his duty, bade fair speedily to become a petty officer. By some means or other he incurred the enmity of a bully, who, by a fawning subservience to his superiors, had been recently made a bos'n's mate, and the climax was reached when Johnston refused to participate in a drunken spree ashore. From that time his life on board became intolerable. Under the cloak of discipline the bos'n's mate seized every possible opportunity to humiliate and insult the young seaman, till one day the young Scot turned upon his tormentor and struck him violently in the face.

The circumstances of this breach of discipline were reported to the Commander, and at the court-martial, where the evidence in support of the prosecution was given by a ship's corporal and two seamen, neither of whom witnessed the assault, the draconic sentence of two years' hard labour, to be followed by dismissal from H.M. service, was passed upon the hapless Scot.

Smarting under the gross injustice of his sentence, Johnston seized the first opportunity of effecting his escape under circumstances of remarkable audacity, and, travelling by night and hiding by day, he made his way towards the coast, trusting to find a sympathetic fisherman to give him a passage away from the danger zone.

Chance led him to the neighbourhood of Polruan, and, as a change of clothes was essential, he resolved to break into a house and procure some garments less distinctive than his own. A fortunate circumstance prompted him to effect an entry into our house.

Now, as it happened, the Brazilian had removed a pane of glass and opened a window barely ten minutes before, and, in order to facilitate his retreat, he had drawn the bolts of both the front and back doors. This he had done without disturbing any of us, and had actually crept into my father's room and removed the cipher from his coat-pocket.

In the meantime the sailor had found the front door ajar and had cautiously made his way into the house, though the slight noise he had made caused me to be on the alert. In the hall he took down an overcoat and hat, but, requiring other articles of clothing, he made up his mind to risk a visit to the upstairs rooms.

Just as he was ascending the stairs he encountered the Brazilian, and, in the darkness, each imagined the other to be one of the occupiers of the house. In almost dead silence they grappled, struggling fiercely and determinedly, till, overbalancing, they both fell in a heap at the foot of the stairs, at the very moment that we were leaning over the balustrades.

Then it was that the Brazilian, whipping out his formidable knife, stabbed the sailor and broke away, only to be "winged" by my uncle's shot.

Thus we were under an obligation to the unfortunate Alec Johnston for his burglarious act. But for him the Brazilian might have got clean away with both the cipher and its key. As far as we knew, he might be an agent for some syndicate of rogues in Pernambuco, who, knowing the history of the "San Philipo," might instantly fit out a vessel to attempt to recover the treasure.

Both my father and his brother expressed themselves very strongly on the subject of the gross injustice done to the young seaman, and, coming to the conclusion that there would be no moral wrong done in concealing the man under these circumstances, they decided to befriend him, or at least to take no active steps in preventing his bid for freedom.

Chapter VI

THE "FORTUNA"

THE next few days were spent in making preliminary plans and preparations for our voyage in search of the "San Philipo" treasure. As I have already stated, the pater had fixed upon most of the details, and he now confided to us the nature of his programme.

Briefly, he proposed to purchase a yacht of sufficient tonnage to make the adventurous passage, yet as small as was compatible with comfort and safety. Seventy tons was the approximate displacement of the vessel he required, and, taking as an example Captain Voss's voyage round the world in the dug-out canoe "Tilikum," Slocum's single-handed cruises across the Atlantic in the comparatively diminutive "Spray," and the instance of a Falmouth quay punt of but thirty feet in length, with a crew of about five hands, making a successful voyage to South Australia, this tonnage should provide an ample margin of safety.

When a suitable vessel had been acquired he proposed to man her with a strong crew, lay in a good supply of stores and salvage gear, and shape a course for the Pacific via the Suez Canal, Indian Ocean, and the Malacca Straits, preferring to take the longer route than to risk the nerve-racking ordeal of a beat round Cape Horn.

Financially we had nothing to fear, for the amount of hard cash received under the terms of Ross Trevena's will would amply cover the expenses of the expedition, and, as the pater remarked with true Cornish philosophy, "as he had never had the making of it he would never miss the spending." In addition, the sudden activity of the Cornish mining industry, had resulted in some shares that my father had in the "Whcal Treganna," and which we had long regarded as a bad investment, rising rapidly considerably, above par, and, by promptly selling out, there was a substantial credit in the family exchequer, so that from a pecuniary point of view our position was a decided improvement to what it had been before Uncle Herbert's hurried trip to Pernambuco.

As a matter of fact, there was no necessity to make this expedition to the far-off Pacific, but so intent was my father on seeing the whole business through (as were my uncle and I), that not for one moment did he swerve from his purpose. "If we find the treasure, as I confidently expect to do, well and good; if we do not, well, at the very least it is a holiday at my uncle Ross Trevena's expense."

With the object of purchasing a suitable craft, a sharp eye was kept on the advertisements in the yachting press, till one day the following announcement caused the pater to make a sudden rush for a railway time-table——

FOR SALE, by order of the executors: The modern 70-ton auxiliary yacht "Fortuna," built 1904 to Lloyd's highest class. Ketch-rigged. Ideal ocean cruiser, fully found, and in perfect condition. Low price to immediate purchaser. Mitcham motor new this year.—Apply Roach & Co., sole agents, Hamble, near Southampton.

"Herbert, old boy," he exclaimed excitedly, "that's just the craft I'm looking for; ketch-rigged—the ideal sail-plan for rough work; 'Mitcham' motor, therefore no risk of being becalmed in the Tropics for weeks at a stretch. When's the next train to Southampton? We'll start at once."

"But why not write for particulars first?" asked my uncle, who, though impetuous, certainly possessed a certain amount of caution.

"And have the yacht snapped up under our very noses? No, no. A well-known firm like Roach & Co. would not deal in rubbish nor act as agents for any craft unless she were exactly as represented. Look sharp and get together what gear you require; and you too, Reggie. Ha, ha! I can already see myself on the deck of the 'Fortuna.'"

"But how about leaving young Johnston?"

"He's able to look after himself now."

"Aren't you afraid he'll clear the place out and make off?"

"Herbert, I don't think I am mistaken. That young fellow could be trusted anywhere. It was his misfortune, not his fault, that first led him into trouble. So I'll trust him, and I'll stake my all that my confidence will not be misplaced."

As the result of my parent's hurried preparations, in less than an hour we were steaming out of Fowey Station in a train which was due at Plymouth in time to catch the 12.18 to Salisbury, a telegram having been dispatched to apprise Roach of our visit.

Throughout the long journey my father, who, much to my surprise, had taken single tickets, was like the proverbial cat on hot bricks. His ill-concealed impatience reminded me forcibly of a child being taken to a toy-shop to purchase a new toy. Uncle Herbert, although also excited, managed to content himself with a couple of newspapers and some weekly journals, though I observed him surreptitiously signing the insurance coupons in the latter. For my part, I was deeply interested in the ever-changing landscape, as the red earth and vivid green foliage of Devon gave place to the dazzling chalk and duller verdure of Dorset and Wilts, till, with remarkable swiftness, the four hours passed and we glided into Salisbury station, from which I had my first glimpse of the slender, needle-like spire of the cathedral.

We made a hasty change of carriages, and, notwithstanding my parent's muttered objurgations on the slowness of the train, it literally crawled into Southampton, where on our arrival I ventured to remind him that we had had nothing to eat since eight that morning—a fact that he, in his excitement, had completely overlooked.

"Grin and bear it, Reggie," he replied. "If we stop here for tea we shall miss the next train to Bursledon. Once there you can eat as much as you like."

It was nearly six when the train drew up at Bursledon, one of the most delightfully situated stations it is possible to imagine. It is perched on the side of a steep hill, with the placid waters of the Hamble River washing the foot of the well-wooded declivity. Notwithstanding the gentle summer's breeze that was swaying the treetops, not a ripple disturbed the surface of the stream, except when an occasional dinghy put off to one or other of the numerous small yachts that swung easily at their moorings. "You ought to have alighted at Netley," remarked the station-master, in reply to an inquiry as to the best means of reaching Hamble village. "But you may possibly get a conveyance, or a boatman down there will row you down-stream."

"Excuse me, sir," exclaimed a tall, bronzed, and bearded individual, rigged out in a tanned jersey, white boating hat, and flannel trousers tucked into a pair of sea-boots, the whole costume liberally bespattered with river mud. "I overheard you say that you wanted to get down to Hamble. My motor-launch is going there in half an hour's time, should you care to take a passage in her."

The pater assented. "It will give us time to get tea," he added. "Where shall we pick up your boat?"

"On the quay by that cottage you can see down there," he replied, pointing to a prettily situated, creeper-covered house close to the water's edge. "We start at seven."

And, touching his hat, the mud-stained individual strolled away with the peculiar slouching gait affected by most seafaring men. "What ought we to give him for the passage down?" asked my father of the station-master, after the motor-boat person had taken his departure. The official smiled in a very amused fashion.

"I don't think I would offer him anything, if I were you," he replied. "He is the Hon. George Pycrust, owner of the steam-yacht 'Chimborazo,' member of the Motor-Yacht Club, and I don't know what else besides. There's no room for snobs on this river, and yachtmen do each other a good turn whenever they have a chance."

We were directed to a little inn on the hill above the railway-station, and here in a few minutes we were enjoying a substantial tea, including a determined attack upon a freshly boiled Warsash crab, a delicacy for which the district is famous, although the flavour is distinctly different from that of the shell-fish caught on our part of the coast.

Punctually at seven o'clock we arrived at the private quay where the Hon. George's motor-launch was waiting, and with the faintest tremor her powerful engine was started and we sped rapidly down the river, my father keeping up an animated conversation with the mud-stained scion of a noble house on the ever-ready subject of yachting.

Quickly the lead-coloured hulks of the obsolete gunboats were left astern, and the three-masted training ship "Mercury" passed, and we came in sight of the red-tiled roofs of Hamble village, fringed with a forest of yachts' masts and backed by a dense mass of trees.

"I'll land you at Roach's private steps," observed our kindly benefactor. "There will be just time to see the 'Fortuna' before dusk. She's a perfect beauty. I came across from Cherbourg in her in a regular sou'-easter, and a better sea boat you could not possibly imagine. If you decide to have her, and keep her in this station, I shall doubtless come across you at times. Here we are. Out fenders and stand by with the boathook," he added, addressing the launch's boy. With scarcely a jar the boat ran alongside the floating landing-stage, and, taking a hearty adieu of the kindly owner, we stepped ashore.

From the pontoon a narrow plank gangway brought us to another broader pier-like structure that ran parallel to the shore over a stretch of soft mud. Here, packed like sardines in a box, were rows of yachts of all sizes and rigs, lying snugly in their mid-berths.

"Ah! Here is Roach, I believe," exclaimed my father, as an alert-looking personage in a yachtsman's uniform came hurrying along the gangway to meet us.

"My name's Trevena. I wired you this morning about the 'Fortuna.' You are Mr. Roach, I presume?"

"The same. We hardly expected so prompt a reply to the advertisement, especially in the shape of a personal call, although we have had several inquiries by letter," replied the yacht-builder, indicating a bundle of communications in his hand. "There is the 'Fortuna'—the fourth yacht in the tier. Would you care to see her now?"

"At once, if you've no objection," replied my father.

"None whatever; everything is open to inspection. I will accompany you, if you like, although most purchasers prefer to make an absolutely private inspection without being influenced by any one interested in the sale."

"Just so. Then we will go alone. Where shall we see you again?"

"I am to be found in that house-boat," he replied, pointing to a large dismasted yacht which had been converted into a floating dwelling.

"Did you ever see such a fine-looking craft?" exclaimed my parent enthusiastically. "Look at her bow—what a fine entry! And what a clean run aft! Get aboard, both of you, as fast as you can." And, scrambling up a narrow swaying plank, we stood on the deck of the yacht "Fortuna."

A flush deck, broken only by a skylight and companion, with fairly high bulwarks fitted with ample scuppers, showed there need be little fear of seas breaking inboard.

For'ard a small booby hatch and a compact yet powerful winch alone encumbered the fo'c'sle deck, while on either side amidships were davits for carrying a gig and a whaler.

A quick yet comprehensive survey of the deck satisfied the pater; then, diving down the companion, with us following closely on his heels, he began a tour of the cabins.

On either side of the companion was a little cabin, comfortable-looking in spite of being dismantled, the one on the starboard side being the owner's, that to the port apparently for the use of a guest.

Both of these opened out of the main saloon, which, with its mahogany swing-table, sideboards, bookcases, and sofa-berths, seemed quite a large apartment compared with the cabin on board our cutter "Spray." This cabin was lighted by the skylight on deck, and at night by a large swinging lamp, judging by the fittings on the deck-beams.

For'ard of the saloon were two small staterooms, separated by a narrow alleyway which gave access to the pantry, captain's cabin, and the fo'c'sle. The latter had accommodation for five men, the iron framework of the folding cots being still in position.

"Plenty of room for a fairly large crew, with slight alterations," remarked my father. "We can easily throw the skipper's cabin and the two staterooms into the fo'c'sle, and make a solid bulkhead across just abaft the pantry."

"Yes, a dozen hands would be comfortably stowed away in that case," replied my uncle. "I suppose you have already made up your mind about her?"

"Nearly."

"Remember the proverb about buying a pig in a poke."

"Also the adage 'Never leave till to-morrow what you can do to-day,'" replied my father, laughing. "Here, give a hand with this trap-hatch, and let's see what she is like."

Underneath the floors the lead ballast had been removed to store, and the timbers and frames carefully cleaned and tarred, so that, as my uncle expressed it, "she was as sweet as new-mown hay." There was no doubt that she had been well looked after. However, the daylight was rapidly fading, so we were forced to bring our investigations to a close, after a hasty inspection of the ladies' cabin abaft the companion.

"Does the 'Fortuna' come up to your expectations?" inquired the yacht-builder when we rejoined him.

"As far as I can judge," replied my father. "Have you an inventory?"

"Here it is, complete in every detail; and you are perfectly at liberty to call in an independent surveyor whenever you like."

"I don't think there is any necessity for that," replied my father. "When could she be ready for sea?"

"We can get her off these next tides—say, the day after to-morrow—and everything could be placed aboard by Thursday night."

"And the price?"

"Seven hundred and fifty pounds; including fitting out."

"Very well, then. We will regard the transaction as completed; allow me to have the use of your office while I write out a cheque."

I doubt whether a yacht had ever before been sold in such a record time; but such was the ease, and before leaving the shipyard we were in possession of the yacht's papers, Mr. Roach having reiterated his promise to have the "Fortuna" ready for sea in four days' time.

I understood now why the pater had taken single tickets; he had set his heart on the "Fortuna" directly he saw the announcement, and had meant to bring her back to Fowey.

The four days, in, spite of the long hours (for we were up from sunrise to sunset), passed very quickly, and, true to his word, Roach had the yacht afloat, her spars varnished and sails bent, the motor reinstalled, and all gear and stores on board within the specified time. No doubt we should have been quite capable of working her home without assistance, but, acting on Uncle Herbert's advice, we engaged a couple of hand's to be on the safe side in case of heavy weather.

Just before ten on the Thursday night the "Fortuna" slipped her moorings and made for the mouth of the river. It was a clear moonlight night, with the faintest suspicion of a breeze from the nor'-east, so the motor was brought into use, and with a gentle purring the powerful little engine urged the yacht through the calm waters of the land-locked estuary.

I remained on deck as we glided down the Solent, with its host of moving lights. We were soon rolling slightly in the tidal race of the Needles Channel. Once clear of the land, we caught the following breeze, and gallantly the ketch responded to the steadily drawing sails.

"Here we are, in the open Channel once more, Reggie," exclaimed my father, who had just relinquished his "trick at the helm" to one of the men. "Hurst Castle light away on our port quarter, the Needles light bears directly astern, and yonder in the distance you can see the flash of St. Catherine's, one of the most powerful lights in the world. See that flash ahead on the starboard bow? That's Anvil Point, on the Dorset coast, so that, provided the weather is clear, navigation on this part of the coast is as safe as can possibly be imagined. We'll have supper now, and then we'll turn in, for it's nearly one o'clock. By the time you are awake I hope we shall be well across West Bay."

So saying, my father took me below, where supper was served in the main saloon. Uncle Herbert had just finished his, and was struggling into his great-coat prior to taking his watch on deck. It was the first time I had seen the cabin by artificial light, and in the swinging rays of the hanging lamp it looked a picture of comfort; the red cushions on the sofa bunks, the thick Turkey carpet on the floor, the curtains across the doors and skylights, and the well-laid swing-table, all combined to make the saloon look a veritable floating home.

"What do you think of it, eh?" asked my father, reading the interested look in my face. "A slight improvement on the 'Spray,' I take it? Well, sit down and make yourself comfortable, for the 'Fortuna's' to be your home for the next eighteen months, I reckon."

Supper over, I turned in on a bunk in the cabin opposite to my father's, which was to be my own, and, lulled by the rhythmical purr of the motor and the gentle undulations of the vessel, I soon fell into a dreamless sleep.

When I awoke it was broad daylight. The yacht was pitching considerably, so that dressing was accomplished under difficulties. Upon going on deck I found my father had already forestalled me, and the meagre crew were engaged in stowing the mizzen, as, owing to the freshening wind, which was coming right aft, it was the canvas which could be most profitably stowed.

It was a grey, misty morning, the sun barely showing through the fleecy clouds overhead. We had just cleared the tail of Portland Race, the, "Bill" showing clearly over our starboard quarter, and the cliffs of West Bay fading away in the haze on our starboard hand. About a mile way to port a large liner was tearing up Channel, and, with a couple of topsail schooners, were the only vessels to be seen.

The compass showed a bearing of S. 84° W., which, allowing for the slight indraught, would bring the yacht close to the Start, although that headland, forty-five miles distant, was, of course, invisible.

"Had a good night, Reggie?" asked my father.

"Splendid!"

"Then you had better go for'ard and get breakfast ready," he replied with a merry laugh. "With so small a crew there can be no idlers, so you must act as steward. But wait till we ship a proper crew, and I'll warrant we'll be as comfortable as at home."

"I notice the motor isn't running."

"No, it would be almost useless in a strong breeze like this; but in a calm it is indispensable. Now cut along and get breakfast; we are all famishing."

I did as I was bid, and the three of us had quite a respectable meal in the saloon, the two hands being left on deck with instructions as to how the yacht's head was to be kept.

After breakfast I went on deck, leaving my father and uncle to overhaul the numerous lockers to become acquainted with their stowage capacity, and to consider the necessity of increasing the space intended for the crew.

About eight o'clock we passed close to a fleet of Brixham trawlers, their rich-coloured tanned sails making a picturesque sight as they beat out towards the trawling grounds. Soon afterwards we sighted the bold headland of Start Point, and with the aid of glass the white lighthouse could be discerned. All this time the "Fortuna" was tearing through the blue water, without the necessity of touching a single sheet or runner, and, provided the wind held, there was a possibility of reaching Fowey before nightfall.

At 1 p.m. the Start was abeam, and here began one of the most interesting stretches of coast that is to be found around the British Isles, and for hours I watched the ever-changing panorama, plying both my father and uncle with numerous questions, and gaining quite a wealth of information about the many noted shipwrecks that have taken place betwixt the Start and the entrance to Plymouth Sound.

We weathered the frowning Bolt Tail just within two hours after leaving the Start, and soon the well-known needle-like shaft of the Eddystone showed up on the sky-line on our port bow.

"Nearly home!" exclaimed Uncle Herbert, indicating the dim outlines of Rame Head. "It's a rattling good passage."

"It will be a bit of a surprise for the fellows at the yacht Club to see the 'Fortuna,' with the club burgee and my house flag flying, bring up in Polruan Pool."

"I think it will be a bigger surprise when she comes back to Fowey with a few tons of silver from the 'San Philipo' lying on her ballast," replied my uncle enthusiastically.

"I hope so," said my father. "Another fortnight will see us under way for Southern seas."

Unfortunately for my father's anticipation, however, the wind fell light, and it was dark before we picked up the friendly gleam of St. Catherine's; and just as the parish church clock was striking midnight the "Fortuna's" anchor fell with a splash and a rattle of chain to the bottom of Fowey Harbour.

Chapter VII

THE EXPEDITION SETS SAIL

WE lost no time in preparing the "Fortuna" for her long voyage, for the morning after her arrival at Fowey my father sent for Clemens, the boat-builder, and instructed him to build a sound-proof bulkhead right across the vessel just abaft the two for'ard state-rooms. These two cabins were then thrown into the fo'c'sle, thus providing six additional bunks; while, to meet the requirements of the increased number of the crew, two large fresh-water tanks were placed below the fo'c'sle floor, and connected with the deck by means of a small pump.

In the meantime my uncle had paid a hurried visit to the Midlands, with the result that five heavy packing-cases arrived at our house. The first contained a three-pounder Q.F. gun, with a light mounting, the second a Maxim with both deck and field mountings, two others contained cases of quick-firing and small-arm ammunition, and the last a number of Lee-Enfield rifles, complete with bayonets, save one, a light sporting rifle. "This is a present for you, Reggie," said my father, placing the latter in my hands. "It is a thoroughly good weapon, and I hope you will appreciate and take great care of it. And, remember, a true sportsman never takes life heedlessly."

"But, pater," I exclaimed, "why do we want such a formidable armoury? Sporting guns I can understand the necessity of; but these are for fighting purposes."

"For defensive purposes," corrected my father. "You remember Findlay's description of the islands in the Pacific where the 'San Philipo's' treasure lies—treacherous and bloodthirsty natives —though, of course, it does not necessarily follow that the arms will be required. We hope and pray they may not be. But forewarned is forearmed, and the moral persuasion of these weapons may have a salutary effect upon any treacherously inclined natives we may. happen to meet."

"But I thought the missionaries had tamed the savage instincts of these natives."

"Without wishing to disparage the splendid work done by the missionaries, Reggie, I can safely assert that on hundreds of these islands cannibalism and the savage rites of heathen worship are as rampant as they were two hundred years ago. It seems remarkable to hear the ideas some people have about foreign parts. Some imagine the Pacific to be a veritable paradise of converted natives clad in gowns of Manchester cotton prints; while, on the other hand, I heard of the case of a youngster going to South Africa to Port Elizabeth, in fact—who took with him a revolver to shoot roaming Kaffirs! To change the subject, would you mind going over to Fowey and getting the *Record*? I've sent an advertisement, and want to make sure that it's in."

In less than an hour I returned with the paper, and this is a copy of my father's announcement—

WANTED.—Twelve ex-naval men to form the crew of an auxiliary yacht about to make a trip round the world. Twelve months' engagement. Must be single men of exemplary character.—Apply by letter, giving full particulars of rating, etc., to Box 1245, office of this paper.

"That's satisfactory," said the pater. "We'll run up to Plymouth to-morrow and call at the *Naval and Military Record* offices, and get the letters."

"So soon?"

"Aye; there'll be a score of replies in the post by now, if I'm not mistaken."

We went to Plymouth as arranged, and, upon calling at the office, we were handed a large wicker tray crammed full with letters and post-cards.

"All these for me?" asked the pater. "Yes, sir, and almost as many again will be in by to-night's post, I daresay."

"Then please destroy the rest, and insert a notice stating that the vacancies have been filled, for I've no doubt that I can suit my requirements from this budget."

From the newspaper office we went to a large firm of provision merchants, and ordered casks and tins of provisions to be sent round to Fowey for shipment on the "Fortuna," and thence to a sailmaker's, where my father ordered a huge square sail to be made to the design which he had drawn.

"What's that for?" I inquired as we left the sail-loft. "The 'Fortuna' does not carry square yards."

"Not at present," replied my father; "but she will do so ere long. I found that on our run down from Hamble, for with the wind dead aft there is always the danger of a gybe with a fore and aft rig, whereas with a square sail the comfort and freedom from mishap is infinitely greater. In the 'Trades' I have no doubt that the sail will be used for days together."

Then twenty suits of clothing for tropical and home use had to be ordered, together with numerous stores from a ship's chandler's, till, almost worn out with the exertions of the day, we returned home—but not to rest, for the huge budget of applications had to be read and classified.

It was a curious mixture. Some letters were well written, others mere scrawl; but the general tone of the whole batch was a willingness to undergo any hardship rather than starve in England.

"Here are a likely dozen," said my father, after perusing nearly a hundred letters. "Tell Johnston to come here and see if he knows any of them."

Johnston, who was making rapid strides towards recovery, had so impressed us with his quiet and orderly demeanour that we had decided to take him with us, placing him on light duties till capable of doing a regular day's work. In response to the summons he came and read down the list of names my father had jotted down.

"No, sir, I don't think I 'know any of them."

"But do you think any of them might know you? It might be awkward, you know."

"I suppose I must take the risk, sir," he replied. "Besides, I shouldn't like my misfortunes to do another man out of a job."

"Very well, then. Here, Herbert, make yourself useful, and write these twelve names on envelopes."

"But, I say——"

"What?"

"Why, with Johnston these twelve will make thirteen—horribly unlucky, you know."

"But we also form part of the crew."

"Not as part of a paid crew."

"Well, to be on the safe side, cut down one," he said with a merry laugh.

So that evening notice that their services were accepted were posted to the men, and the crew of the "Fortuna" was as follows:—

Captain: HOWARD TREVENA, R.N.R.
Mate: HERBERT TREVENA, R.N.R.
Second Mate: REGINALD TREVENA.
Boatswain: PETER WILKINS, late bos'n's mate, R.N.
Quartermaster: TRESCO LORD, late master-at-arms.
Deck hands:—

ROBERT DALLEY, late armourer, R.N.

WM. STAINER, late armourer, R.N.

EDWARD HINKS, late gunner's mate, R.N.

FREDK MONEY, late gunner's mate, R.N.

WM. LEWIS, A.B., late seaman diver, R.N.

GEORGE BURBIDGE, A.B., late seaman diver, R.N.

JOSEPH DIRHAM, A.B.

JOHN MILLS, A.B.

FREDK. BARNES, A.B.

ALEC JOHNSTON, A.B. (to act as officers' steward).

In spite of the greatest secrecy on our part, rumours of the object of the voyage began to get about, older people naturally and correctly associating the almost forgotten "San Philipo" treasure with the expedition, greatly to my father's anger. However, we managed to get the arms and ammunition on board, lowering the gun by means of tackle from our garden into a boat which we brought alongside at high water, working as silently as we could in the dead of night.

By Saturday the last of the stores was aboard, including two diving suits from Siebe, Gorman & Co., and all that remained was to fill up the tanks with fresh water and ship the crew.

The latter had been told to assemble at the railway-station at 10 a.m. on Monday, and thither my uncle and I repaired to muster the men and take them to the vessel. To our surprise we found that, long before the arrival of the train, four men were already on the platform, having tramped from Plymouth, over twenty-seven miles of hilly road, for want of sufficient money to pay their railway fares.

The arrival of the train brought the rest of the contingent—not a man was missing—and, led by my uncle and myself, the whole party marched in an orderly manner down the narrow Fore Street, to the undisguised astonishment of the townsfolk. In their civilian clothing the men looked a nondescript lot, some bearded, some clean-shaven, and a few, departing from the naval custom, had grown moustaches, while each man carried either a bundle tied up in a blue handkerchief or else a black ditty-box under his arm. Nevertheless, they were a fine body of active, middle-aged men, and, with their previous training, would soon fall into regular sea-going routine.

Outside the "King of Prussia" the party was joined by my father, who led the men into a room where a well-laid breakfast awaited them. This they did full justice to, the need of a good meal being apparently no stranger to the majority of them.

Then my father addressed them. It was the first time I had heard him speak in public, and the warmth and earnestness of his words astonished me. He began by telling the men plainly that the voyage was to be no mere pleasure-trip, but occasional hard work was required, and even actual danger might have to be faced. On the other hand, the "Fortuna," though small, was exceptionally seaworthy, and everything that could be done for their comfort had been provided. He even hinted at an additional reward for their services should the voyage come up to anticipations, although he stated distinctly, that he gave no definite promise on that account, and finally explained that any man who wished to withdraw could do so, and his fare to and from his home would be paid forthwith.

However, our new crew were unanimous in their choice, and the signing of the men's papers was proceeded with. Then the party marched down to Whitehouse Steps, where the watermen rowed them off to the "Fortuna."

The rest of the day was spent in getting the men accustomed to the vessel. Proper watches were set, the starboard watch under my father and the bos'n, the port watch under Uncle Herbert and the quartermaster, and ship's time took the place of shore time, the hours and half-hours being sounded by the bell.

At four in the afternoon—or eight bells, as I should have expressed it—we went ashore to our home in Polruan. All arrangements had been made for the proper care of the home during our absence, and the remainder of the day was spent in receiving our numerous friends who had come over to bid us farewell and good luck; for, now that the final details had been completed, there was little need to conceal the fact that the "San Philipo" treasure was, as had been conjectured, the object of our voyage.

It was nightfall ere we left the house for the last time for a good many months. At Polruan Quay the gig awaited us, and, urged by the powerful strokes of the rowers, the little craft was soon alongside the "Fortuna." In true nautical style the shrill pipe of the bos'n's whistle was heard, and the crew stood to attention as the yacht's officers came on board. Then, directly the gig was hoisted in the davits, the crew returned to their stand-easy on the fo'c'sle, the dancing beams of the anchor light and the glowing bowls of the men's pipes dimly illuminating the shadowy forms of the seamen, as in low tones they discussed the projects of the voyage or talked reminiscently of bygone commissions.

"I don't think you will ever be dull during the voyage, Reggie," remarked my father, indicating the knot of men with a wave of his hand. "Amongst that little crew there is to be gathered a wealth of adventure from all the five oceans. And some of their yarns are well worth listening to, I can assure you."

At ten o'clock the following morning my father was rowed ashore to obtain the necessary ship's papers from the Custom-house, and half an hour later the "Fortuna" slipped her moorings, and, dipping her ensign as a farewell salute to the Yacht Club, glided swiftly out of Fowey Harbour on her long voyage to the coral islands of the Pacific.

Half an hour later the grim outlines of the Gribben were lost to sight in the mist that overhung the land, and, with every sail drawing, the "Fortuna" rapidly drew away from the shores of dear old England.

Chapter VIII

A RESCUE AT SEA

"THERE'S a power o' wind behind that mirk, sir," exclaimed Wilkins, the bos'n, jerking his thumb in the direction of the dark, ill-defined clouds that had shut out the sight of land.

"Yes, we are in for a good dusting," replied my father. "The glass is rising far too rapidly. Make everything secure on deck, and put extra lashings on the boats. And also," he added, as the bos'n saluted and began to make his way for'ard, "have the jibs changed before it gets too thick."

We were sufficiently far from land to prevent its affording much shelter, and with the increasing wind, huge waves began to curl viciously under our counter, threatening every moment to break over our quarter. But the staunch little yacht rose splendidly to each white crest, and, beyond a shower of spray that darkened our canvas almost to the peak, hardly a drop of solid water reached our decks. Astern, the trailing line of the Walker "Cherub" log was stretched to almost the rigidity of an iron bar, and the indicator bell, sounding at every quarter-knot with less than two minutes' interval, showed our speed to be well over seven knots.

Suddenly, accompanied by a blinding downpour of hail that rolled on our decks and clustered in white patches in our lee scuppers, a furious squall struck us, making the "Fortuna" heel till I thought she would never recover herself. But with a few rapid turns of the wheel the helm was put hard up, till, relieved of the enormous pressure on her canvas, the yacht shook herself free like a great mastiff emerging from the water.

"Pay her head off a point now," shouted the bos'n to the seaman at the wheel, and, without losing way, the yacht resumed her course, churning the sea over her bows in swishing columns of spray.

While the squall lasted, I was dimly aware that I was gripping a belaying-pin like grim death, swallowing mouthfuls of salt-laden air, till it seemed that I was actually enveloped in water, while each wave, as it flung itself against our quarter, shook the bulwarks till it threatened to tear them bodily away.

In obedience to an order that was inaudible to me, several of the crew came rushing along the deck, in spite of the terrific heel and jerky motion of the vessel, and in a few moments the halliards of the mainsail were paid out, and a dozen strong hands were struggling with the cringles and reef-points of the mainsail. Directly the reef was "knocked down," the "Fortuna" took things easier, yet with apparently undiminished speed she threshed her way through the foam-crested waves.

"Sail on the port bow, sir," repeated the bos'n, taking up the cry from a seaman on the look-out for'ard; and through the driving rain we could see a large topsail schooner, her close-reefed mainsail streaming in ribbons, and only her foresail and inner jib set, pounding heavily on the port-tack, the waves sweeping clean over her sides, as, high in ballast, she listed dangerously, till one could almost fancy that her weather bilges were showing.

"There's an old coffin!" shouted Uncle Herbert in my ear. "Four times our size and nothing like so seaworthy."

"It's an absolute scandal to allow a ship to put to sea so high in ballast," bawled my father, who overheard the remark. "If they insist on a Plimsoll line to prevent overloading, why not a similar mark to stop vessels putting to sea too light?"

"I don't know," replied my uncle, shaking the water from his sou'-wester. "But yonder craft will be lucky if ever she makes port in safety. Look at her now."

An extra vicious blast had come, sweeping down, making even the "Fortuna," with her double-reefed canvas, reel; but the schooner staggered as if struck by a solid substance, and heeled over till her topsail yards almost touched the water, and I thought she had actually capsized.

At length she slowly righted, and, staggering and plunging, she was soon lost to sight in the rain-laden atmosphere.

Shortly afterwards two torpedo-boat destroyers came thrashing along within a cable's length of our stern, their four squat funnels, caked white with salt, belching out volumes of black smoke, through which gleamed dark red flames, the indications of steaming under forced draught. There was no attempt on the part of these dogs of war to ride the waves: their sharp bows simply cut through the heaving water, which fell in cascades from their turtle-back decks. On either bridge could be discerned the glistening sou'-westers of the officers on duty, as, to avoid the blinding spray, they crouched behind the storm-dodgers, while, as the destroyers tore past, we had a momentary glimpse of their weather-worn white ensigns, and both craft were hidden in a chaos of spray and smoke.

"You had better get below and have something to eat," shouted my father; but I shook my head.

"A bit queer, eh?"

"No," I replied, conscious at the same time that I did feel a trifle uneasy.

"Then cut off down below," he repeated, "and keep out of the wet for a time. Tell Johnston to make you some tea; you look pinched with cold."

I obeyed, and, staggering across the slippery deck, I gained the companion and reached the shelter of the saloon. The place was in semi-darkness, for dead-lights had been placed over the scuttles and the skylight covered over with tarpaulins, and the only illumination was the dim daylight that filtered through the half-closed companion hatch. Coming from the open air, the atmosphere of the saloon seemed close and oppressive, and I would have willingly preferred to remain on deck during the storm (which Uncle Herbert insisted on terming a strong breeze) rather than be cooped up 'tween decks.

However, I lay down on one of the sofa-bunks on the lee side, battling with a dizzy sensation that made me lose all interest in life; but I could remember watching the antics of the swing table as it oscillated, in spite of its construction, with the pitching of the vessel, and wondering whether, a soda-water siphon, that was continually sliding from one side of the table to the other, would overbalance and explode.

How long I remained thus I have no idea, though it may have been hours; but suddenly there was a hurried trampling of feet on deck, a succession of orders, and the "Fortuna" went about on the other tack, sending me flying from the berth (which was now on the weather side) on to the floor, where I lay, covered with cushions, books, and half-a-dozen wooden boxes which had been disgorged from a cupboard through the lock being insecurely fastened.

In an instant my scattered senses returned, and, realizing that something unusual must have happened for the yacht to be put on the other tack when she was sailing free on her proper course, I sprang to my feet and scrambled up the companion.

On gaining the deck I found the crew clustered along the lee bulwarks, gazing intently upon a small craft barely a hundred yards away. It was a yacht, apparently, of about three or four tons, with a large rent in her mainsail, her storm-jib in ribbons, and only her foresail intact.

As she fell into the trough of the huge seas she lost the wind, but the moment she rose on the crest of a wave she was caught by the furious gusts and heeled till we could almost see her keel and as she heeled a long dark line showed on her white side close to her chain plates.

"She's done for!" shouted the bos'n. "That last squall has burst one of her seams." Crouched in her cockpit was a man whose white face was drawn with the peril of the situation. With one hand he grasped the tiller, and with the other he appeared to be trying to pump out the water that was pouring into the doomed craft, occasionally desisting to wave a frantic appeal for assistance.

Snatching a lifebuoy, my uncle rapidly bent a stout grass line to it, and held it up for the unfortunate yachtsman to see, for shouting was useless. In another moment the "Fortuna," which was tearing through the water like a racehorse, had left the disabled craft far astern.

"Lee ho!" shouted the bos'n, and with a loud flapping of canvas the "Fortuna" ran up into the wind, and, drawing on the other tack, ran back on her errand of mercy. In spite of the sheets being slacked well off, our stout little craft rushed towards the unfortunate yacht, our intention being to pass as close to windward of her and as slowly as possible, and to try and pick up the stranger with the lifebelt, for any attempt at luffing would entail great risks to us should the "Fortuna" drift or fall foul of the almost waterlogged craft.

It seemed but a few seconds before we were again abreast of the disabled yacht. My uncle, springing on to the lee bulwarks and steadying himself with his left hand round the shrouds, poised the lifebelt with his right, and prepared to make a cast.

"Jump for it! We'll pick you up!" shouted the men in a chorus, for we were passing within a few yards of the stranger.

The man stood upright, and made ready to spring, but at the crucial moment he hesitated, and the opportunity had passed. Even as he returned to his former position in the cockpit, the little craft flung her stern high out of the water, and with a splash and a turmoil of escaping air she disappeared beneath the waves.

There was a general groan of dismay from the crew; then suddenly I heard my father shout, "What's that man doing? Stop him, you fellows!" But, before any one could raise a hand, one of the crew had torn off his oilskins, flung a lifebelt overboard, and had plunged in after it.

Instantly there was a rush towards the whaler. The crew stood by the falls and waited for the order; but my father, glancing at the mountainous waves, bade them desist.

"They must take their chance," he shouted. "The boat could never live in such a sea. Up aloft one of you and keep a bright look-out. Lee, ho! Hard down with your helm!"

The "Fortuna" flung about on the other tack, and with the ropes coiled ready to throw to their comrade and the unfortunate yachtsman, our crew anxiously awaited their opportunity.

One man with the agility of a monkey had swung himself aloft, and was perched on the crosstrees. He shouted, but his voice was inaudible, though by his gestures we knew that one at least of the men had been sighted.

"Bear away a bit! Steady!"

Following the direction indicated by the look-out, I saw a dark object on the crest of a wave. The next moment it was lost to sight in the trough, but on the summit of the next roller I could make out the head and shoulders of the yachtsman encircled by the lifebelt, and our brave seaman steadying himself with one hand on the belt and keeping afloat as unconcernedly as if in a swimming bath.

"Bear away a bit more! Stand by there, men!" shouted my father. "Be sharp with those bowlines and haul them up roundly directly they catch them!"

"Let's hope the poor fellow has strength to hold on," he added to his brother. "I am afraid we are carrying too much way; yet if we luff her, she will roll over on top of them and crush their skulls like egg-shells."

"We must risk it. It's their only chance," replied my uncle.

"Very well, then, I will," said my father, and, raising his voice, he gave the order: "Luff her up!"

Quivering like a wounded animal, the "Fortuna" ran up into the wind, with sufficient way to bring, her up to the two well-nigh exhausted men. One of the crew stationed at the main chains threw a bowline. It missed, but the second was more successful, for it fell over the shoulders of the stranger, and as the man paid out the line handsomely a wave swept the unfortunate man against the ship's side, raising him to within reach of half-a-dozen willing hands on deck. At the same instant his rescuer grasped the bowline, and, with great presence of mind, thrust his feet through the loop, and amid the cheers of the crew both men were hauled over the side.

"Take both of them down to the saloon," said my father, "and tell Johnston to get some hot water ready as soon as possible."

"Fire's out, sir," replied one of the crew. "We had to unship the galley funnel."

"Then re-ship the funnel, and rig preventer stays to it. Should it be carried away it can't be helped; if not, so much the better."

"Very good, sir."

"And what's this man's name?" asked my parent, indicating the gallant rescuer, who was being assisted down the companion.

"Lewis, sir; Bill Lewis."

"Capital fellow! Capital fellow!" exclaimed my father; and, having seen that the "Fortuna" once more lay on her proper course, he went down into the saloon, I following him.

The excitement of the last half-hour had driven away all feelings of sea-sickness, and, strangely enough, I felt no discomfort at being in the cabin. The rescued yachtsman was lying motionless on one of the berths, his body enveloped in blankets. I noticed that there was a clean cut on his cheek, extending from the right ear nearly to the chin, which had bled freely; and I also remarked that his hands, though hardened by manual labour, were well cared for. Apparently he had not swallowed much sea water, for he was sleeping soundly as if tired out with sheer exhaustion.

His rescuer, Lewis, was little the worse for his gallant efforts, and was sitting awkwardly in a deck chair as if out of place in the saloon of a yacht.

He rose as my father entered the cabin, and shuffled with his feet in his embarrassment.

"I am proud of you, Lewis!" exclaimed my father, shaking him by the hand.

"'Twas nothing, sir."

"It was a gallant deed."

"May be, sir; but I didn't stop to think. If I did I mightn't have gone overboard."

"I'll not forget it, Lewis. I hope to send a report of your bravery to the proper quarter at the first opportunity. Is there anything I can do for you now?"

"No, sir, not as I knows of. Leastways, I'd like to go for'ard and have a pipe. I'm just longing for a draw."

"Certainly, Lewis; but how did you get that bruise?" added the pater, noticing the man's eye, which was considerably damaged and rapidly turning a greenish black.

"While I was in the water, sir. Directly I saw the gent yonder I swam for him, pushing the lifebelt afore me. Then I bore in mind the instructions for saving drowning persons, to assure him with a loud and firm voice that he was safe, though I'll allow my voice didn't strike me as being particularly loud and firm, and neither did I feel so very sure that he was safe. However, I did as was directed, and, getting up behind him, I tugged at his hair to turn him on his back. It's all very fine a-laying down regulations for saving a man, but I reckon the fellow as wrote 'em never had to do the trick hisself, for directly I laid hold of the young gent he twists round somehow and plugs me in the eye. So I had to let go, and down he went again. The next time he came up I pitched the belt over his head, and he grabbed at it like grim death.

"After a bit he quieted down somewhat, and I took hold of the lifebelt too, as I began to feel done up. There was no sign of the ship, and I thought she had missed us and that I had lost the number of my mess; but soon afterwards I saw her bearing down, and we were taken aboard."

"Well, let's be thankful it's no worse," remarked my father, smiling. "Now cut away for'ard and enjoy your smoke, and tell the bos'n that it's your watch below to-night."

"Thank'ee, sir," said Lewis, saluting and backing out of the saloon as if thankful for his release.

In obedience to an order, three of the seamen carried the still sleeping yachtsman into my cabin and placed him in bed.

"He'll be comfortable there, Reggie," remarked the pater. "And you can sleep on the spare bunk in my cabin to-night. To-morrow we may no doubt hear an interesting story of his adventures. Now, tell Johnston to hurry up with the dinner."

Chapter IX

AN ADDITION TO THE CREW

BY daybreak on the following morning the gale had moderated, and, the wind being dead aft, the mainsail and mizzen had been stowed and the square sail set.

We had passed Ushant light during the night and were now well into the Bay.

When I came on deck there was nothing to be seen save an unbroken waste of water; although the waves were not so high nor so steep, they were of great distance from crest to crest, as, with unfailing regularity, they rolled into the Bay from the vast Atlantic.

After breakfast I went into my cabin to see how the rescued man was progressing. He was asleep, but while I was engaged in taking some articles from a drawer he awoke with a sudden start and sat up in his bunk.

"Where am I?" he asked.

"On board the yacht 'Fortuna.'"

"How did I get here? Ah! I remember."

"How do you feel this morning?" I inquired politely. "Is there anything you require?"

"I should like something to drink, for my throat is like a limekiln. What's this?" he added, placing his hand over his bandaged face. "Have I had a cut?"

"Yes, a slight one," I replied. "Take it easy, and I'll send Johnston in with your breakfast."

I went out, and, having told our steward to take the stranger a good meal, I rejoined the pater and informed him that the man was awake.

"What are we going to do with him?" I asked.

"Put him aboard the first homeward-bound vessel we speak to, or else land him at Gib. Poor fellow, he's had a narrow squeak, but I cannot for the life of me understand why foolhardy fellows persist in taking, single-handed, risks in small yachts. When we had the 'Spray,' keeping in sight of land was good enough for me, and then only with a sharp eye on the barometer. Where he came from and where he was making for seems a mystery, but I suppose we shall know before long."

"How far have we come?" I asked, as I saw my father examine the indicator of the log.

"A hundred and fifty-six miles in twenty-three hours."

"And how far before we sight land?"

"Roughly, it is three hundred miles to Cape Finisterre, and then we shall be practically in sight of land right round the coast of Portugal and Spain till we reach Gib."

"And where's Uncle Herbert? I haven't seen him this morning."

"But haven't you heard him? It's his watch below, and most likely he's sound asleep and snoring. But look, here's a sight for you."

Rapidly bearing down towards us was a huge liner, her graceful hull glistening in the sunlight as she thrashed her way through the water. As she drew nearer we could see her decks crowded with passengers, who were regarding, doubtless with considerable curiosity, our little strangely rigged craft as she ploughed her way over the rollers.

We dipped our ensign, and in reply the liner's flag was slowly lowered and as slowly rehoisted, and twenty minutes later she was a mere speck on the horizon.

Soon afterwards the rescued yachtsman appeared' on deck, assisted by Johnston, and, making his way towards us, warmly thanked my father for saving his life. "You certainly were in a bit of a pickle," remarked my pater, offering him a deck-chair and producing his cigar-case. "Let's hear all about it, for, with pardonable curiosity, I am eager to learn the facts of the case."

"With pleasure, Mr. Trevena. You see, I obtained your name from the steward, and have gathered some particulars about the 'Fortuna.' But to proceed to the story of my adventures. My name is Arthur Conolly, by profession I am a doctor of medicine, by choice I would be a yachtsman, for the sea always had a strong attraction for me. When at home I live in Dublin—or 'dear dirty Dublin,' as my compatriots fondly term it—but on every suitable opportunity I cruise around the British Isles in my three-tonner 'Sea Shell,' or rather, I should say, I cruised, for my snug little craft is unfortunately at the bottom of the sea.

"On Monday last I left Wexford Harbour, intending to fetch Falmouth and thence by easy stages round the Solent, where I have invariably spent the months of July and August during the past seven years. The 'Sea Shell' is, or was, a modern type of boat, with spoon bow and short counter, and a short keel. She had a watertight cockpit, and was in every way fitted for single-handed work, except for one thing: she would not lie hove-to without constant attention, a fault which the older type of straight-stemmed boats never possessed; and that defect was the cause of my misfortune.

"All went well till I had reeled off a hundred and sixty miles by the log and had sighted the Wolf on my port bow. The glass had been very irregular during the last twelve hours, but just before nightfall it came on to blow hard from the north-west. Knowing I was in the vicinity of the dangerous Scilly Islands, I bore up to the south'ard, intending to give them a wide berth before heading up Channel, but about two in the morning the squalls were so frequent and violent that I threw out a sea-anchor.

"Daylight showed that I was within five miles of St. Agnes, and the wind having veered to the north'ard I knew that I was comparatively safe and was in no danger of being cast ashore, though the shift of wind had knocked up a nasty cross-sea.

"However, for six hours the 'Sea Shell' rode to the sea-anchor, but about noon, while I was down below having something to eat, the yacht's motion became so erratic, and such heavy seas tumbled on her decks, that I knew something had gone wrong.

"Upon going on deck, I found, to my horror, that the riding-rope of the sea-anchor had chafed through, and consequently, the anchor being lost, the yacht was aimlessly tossing in the crested seas. Only one thing remained to be done: to show the merest spread of canvas and try and gain the shelter of the land. I managed, although I was frequently up to my waist in water, to hoist the reefed foresail, and, the yacht's head having been paid off, I thereupon began to set the close-reefed mainsail. Hardly had I hoisted the throat than an extra strong squall struck the boat, and in a moment the mainsail had burst right along the dentre-cloths. Nevertheless I set the storm-jib, and by dint of careful nursing I managed to keep a small amount of way on, though every time the 'Sea Shell' rose on the crest of a wave she was nearly knocked on her beam ends by the force of the wind.

"Then I tried to lay her to, but she yawed to such an extent that that manoeuvre was impossible, so I had to let her go, handling her as gently as I could for fear of carrying away the gear.

"This went on for several hours, and though the watertight cockpit was continually getting full of water, it drained out without a drop getting below. After a time, however, I realized that the 'Sea Shell' was not so buoyant as she had been, and that she plunged sluggishly into the crests of the waves, and on looking down the hatch I found that the cabin floor was awash, and the yacht was slowly, yet none the less surely, foundering.

"Then, for the first time, I realized the absolute danger of my position. During the terrible buffeting she had received, the 'Sea Shell' had opened a seam, and the cabin being panelled, it was impossible to caulk the leak from the inside, even had the yacht been capable of being hove-to for a sufficient time to effect the repairs.

"Under these circumstances I was helpless. At one time I thought seriously of cutting away the mast and gear, and riding to the wreckage as to a sea-anchor, but the almost certainty of having more planks stove in by the mast before I could get it clear made me abandon that plan. So I set to work at the pump, hoping that I might keep down the leak until, perhaps, some passing vessel might sight me, or even—vain hope—that, even though there was no sign of the coast, I might gain the lee of the land before the little craft sank under me."

"It seemed hours, though in reality it must have been less than an hour, before I was compelled through sheer exhaustion to desist, and upon looking round, hoping against hope to see a friendly sail, I found that your yacht was close to windward of me, and the rest you know."

"Don't you think you tempted Providence once too often?" asked my father. "After all, long single-handed cruises may be considered smart in their way, but are they worth the risk?"

"No more risky than ballooning, mountaineering, or, if it comes to that, playing football or cycling."

"No man could be keener on sailing than I am, but I would think twice ere I made a long cruise in a craft like yours. I certainly admire your pluck, but at the same time I think you ran a needless risk."

"A man can only die once."

"That, if I may be allowed to say so, is a foolish expression, and one that one hears from unthinking individuals after they have safely passed through danger. I will explain what I mean. You are still a young man, I believe?

"Thirty years of age."

"Then, taking a moderate estimate, you are good for another thirty years."

"From a medical point of view, I should say yes."

"Then, had you gone down with your yacht it necessarily follows that you would have, through your own rashness, thrown away thirty years of a pleasurable existence. I, for instance, am fifteen years older than you are, but I still call myself young for all that; and I can assure you that, unless a man realizes that he must make the very best of life, his mission on earth is wasted. How many instances are there of people living in hope of having a 'good time' at some future period of their existence who fail to appreciate their present position, and so waste their lives in a miserable longing for the unattainable. Now, Mr. Conolly, I hope you will excuse my lecturing you, but from the nature of your remark I found it impossible to let the opportunity pass; but we will now change the subject."

For some time my father and the doctor talked about a variety of topics, and I could see that Mr. Conolly grew deeply interested when the nature of our cruise was told him.

"I have just mentioned to my son," said the pater, "that I propose transferring you to a homeward-bound ship or else landing you at Gib. Naturally we could not beat back fifty miles or so against half a gale to set you ashore at Falmouth, so you must be our guest, willing or unwilling, for the next few days."

"I am deeply obliged to you," replied the doctor; "but pardon me if I make a suggestion that may not meet with your approval. Like most Irishmen, I am a man actuated by sudden impulses. My proposition is this: You have no medical man on board, and you are bound for the tropics. I am a fully qualified doctor and could be handy to you in more ways than one. Why not allow me to fill the post of medical officer? As a matter of fact, I have been promised a berth in a big steamship company in a year's time, so that the cruise would help pass the time in a most pleasant and instructive manner. I would ask no remuneration, save my rations and clothing, for, as you know, all I possess at the present moment is the clothes I wore when I was hauled on board. Now, Mr. Trevena, what do you think of my proposal?"

"Rather sudden, isn't it?" replied my father, laughing. "Well, well; I must see what my brother has to say about it first, though personally I think it an admirable arrangement."

So saying, the pater went below to arouse his sleeping brother; but apparently they soon came to an understanding, for within five minutes he returned on deck.

"Herbert is delighted at the suggestion. He always was a livery subject in hot weather," said my father. "So you can consider yourself one of the officers of the 'Fortuna.' I think you had better stick to the cabin you slept in last night, and Reggie will have to make the best of it."

"I don't mind, father," I exclaimed.

"It wouldn't matter if you did," returned the pater dryly. "But there is one condition I must make, Mr. Conolly."

"And that is——?"

"On board this yacht we all, officers and men, mean to be as comfortable as we possibly can, so there is one topic of conversation, and one only, that I must ask you to avoid. As you are of Hibernian birth I am afraid you will find it difficult to do so."

"Then what is it?" said the doctor, with a slight trace of anxiety on his features.

"Politics," replied my father, with a chuckle.

Chapter X

YARNS IN THE FIRST WATCH

AT midnight on the third day after passing Ushant we had crossed the Bay, and the white flashing light on Cape Finisterre showed abeam. During the night the wind had fallen, but at daybreak a fresh off-shore breeze had sprung up, enabling us to make rapid progress under all plain sail.

Throughout the day we were in sight of the ironbound coast, which from a distance presented an uninviting aspect. Owing to the abundance of pyrites along the cliffs there is said to be a danger of great deviation of the compass, and in our case we found, by taking a series of azimuths and amplitudes, that such was the case.

Fortunately, there was no sign of mist, so that a compass course was not absolutely necessary; but that evening the wind fell almost to a dead calm, and the darkness was so intense that the "Fortuna's" head was placed a point off the recognized course to prevent possible accidents.

It was a glorious night. The air was soft and balmy, and, though there were no stars visible, there was a curious phosphorescence on the water that compensated for the inky darkness of the atmosphere. In fact, it was the first evening of the voyage that could be termed splendid, and at dinner in the saloon we had skylights and ports opened to admit the air.

Presently came the sound of stringed instruments played with decided skill and expression. We looked at one another with astonishment, for music was one of the last things we expected to hear.

"Mr. Wilkins!" called my uncle through the skylight.

"Aye, aye, sir," replied the bos'n, descending the companion.

"What's that noise?"

"The watch below have got up a small band," explained the bos'n. "Shall I pass the word for them to knock off?"

"Oh, no; far from it," said my father. "But where on earth did they get the instruments from?

"Made 'em from 'baccy-boxes and bits of wire, sir. It's an old seaman's trick."

"They play jolly well," rejoined my father. "I'll tell you what. We'll have a concert on deck to-night; it will please the men. Pass the word, Mr. Wilkins."

The bos'n retired, and presently a hoarse cheer announced that the skipper's message had been welcomed by the men; and after dinner the fo'c'sle, illuminated with several lamps, was crowded with the crew, who sat on inverted tub's, coils of rope, etc., while the officers were provided with chairs from the saloon.

It seemed really marvellous what music could be obtained from such primitive instruments as the men had constructed, and, stranger still, the almost boyish delight that the grown-up men—with one exception all over forty—took in the rough-and-ready concert.

The items were mostly from the old sea stock, chanties and Dibdin's songs predominating. The bos'n led off with "Barney Buntline," and although his version of the words varied somewhat from the original, the chorus was taken up right lustily by nearly a score of voices, till some belated peasant on the Iberian shore must have wondered at the strange noise that came from the sea.

> Then often have we seamen heard
> How men are killed and undone
> By overturns of carriages
> And fires and thieves in London.
> Bow, bow, bow; rum (give it tongue, lads),
> Bow, bow, bow...

The men repeated the chorus till I felt sure their throats ached; but, nothing daunted, they gave "Sally Brown" in approved chanty style, followed by a quick-step on their stringed instruments.

"The Anchor's Weighed" and "All's Well" followed in quick succession, and Dr. Conolly contributed a stump speech with a Hibernian twang that evoked such rounds of applause that he was compelled to give what the men, termed "a hancore."

Several other items also received tremendous applause, The Old Folks at Home being given with such fervour that one would imagine that every man of the crew had near relations in England, instead of which they were practically without kith or kin; and just before six bells "God Save the King" brought the concert to a close, the men standing with heels together and heads bared in an attitude of devoted and simple loyalty.

At daybreak on the twelfth day of the voyage the "Fortuna" arrived at Gibraltar, entering the harbour under power, this being the first time the motor had been utilized since leaving Fowey. We anchored to the south'ard of the Rosia Mole, but hardly was everything made snug when a naval picket-boat steamed off, informing us that we were in the Admiralty anchorage grounds. So the anchor had to be weighed and the "Fortuna" moved to a spot pointed out by the lieutenant of the naval boat, close to the neutral ground, with the Devil's Tower just showing clear of Mala Point.

Here we were immediately surrounded by a swarm of bumboatmen, who offered us all kinds of articles, from bread to copper paint, and from copper paint back to bread; but by liberal speech the bos'n and the quartermaster cleared them away. The gig was lowered and manned and we went ashore, where I made my first acquaintance with a foreign port; for though under the British flag, Gibraltar is essentially "foreign" in appearance, language, and customs.

Having obtained a clean "bill of health," the next business was to order stores and water, and for the first time I realized the value of that precious fluid, which, though excessively dear, was dirty and not particularly sweet.

Two days later the "Fortuna" left Gib, and with a light easterly breeze she passed through the Straits under sail and power.

"Why have we the motor running, as the wind is aft?" I asked my father.

"Because we want to get through the Straits before the tidal stream changes."

"But we are in the Mediterranean Sea now, are we not? I thought the Mediterranean was tideless."

"Yes, so it is; but there is a strong tidal current—which is a very different thing from a tide—running under us now at the rate of nearly six knots. In another two hours it will change and be against us. If the Straits were wide enough to admit the progress of the tidal wave there would be a rise and fall in the ports of the Mediterranean, but as they are not, only the tidal current rushes in and out twice every day."

For seven days we kept in sight of the African shore, our rate of progression averaging ninety-five miles per diem, and as luck would have it, we missed the gales so prevalent off the Algerian coast, the weather being balmy by day and cool at night.

On the second night after leaving Gibraltar, I strolled for'ard to where a group of sailors were sitting on the fo'c'sle telling yarns.

"I hope you won't mind my listening," I said apologetically. "I should like a good yarn, so carry on, just as if I were not here."

"Carry on, Joe!" exclaimed one of the men. "You were just a-goin' to spin that yarn about the ghost of the 'M———'s' cat."

"I heard about that yarn when I was in the Channel Fleet," said another, who had just joined the group, and was busily engaged in ramming black tobacco into a still blacker clay pipe. "An' much as I likes Joe Dirham, I shall be obliged to tell 'im he's a liar if he persists in spinning that cuffer."

"'Tain't no more a cuffer than you are, Fred Money, for, as true as I sits 'ere, I was the man who saw it."

"What! You saw it."

"Yes."

"Joe," exclaimed his chum, in a mournful voice, "is it only plain water that you drank with your supper?"

"Never mind him, Joe," chimed in another, "but fire away."

"Well, when I was in the 'M———' in '91— she was a rotten old gunboat that would drift to loo'ard as fast as she would steam ahead—we left Portsmouth for Portland with a lot of diving gear for the Channel Fleet. It was Christmas Eve, and snowing like anything, I remember. Just as we had cleared the Needles, the old man called me —he was a Warrant Officer in charge—and says, 'Dirham, there's a blessed cat in my cabin. Get hold of her and pitch her overboard or she'll get hold of my canaries,' for he used to keep a couple of 'em caged up. Well, I grabs hold of this 'ere cat, and the brute makes for me and bites my finger. Although I was precious sorry for the animal, orders is orders, but before slinging it overboard I hits it behind the ear with a bit of iron bar, and stunned it. Then I lashes the iron on to its neck and over the side it goes.

"Back I goes to the old man's cabin. 'All correct, sir,' I reports. 'Very well, carry on,' ses 'e, 'but first 'ave a glass of rum.' Believe me, as I was drinking that, and the old man was sitting in his easy-chair with his legs on the fender, of the stove, that blessed cat, or its ghost, walked out from behind the sideboard, slipped over my boots and under the old man's legs, and disappeared under the bunk.

"My eyes were nearly startin' out of my 'ead, and I all but dropped the glass on to the floor. 'What's this, you lying rascal?' roars the old man. 'What do you mean by sayin' that you drowned that cat?' 'So I did, sir,' I answered, and told 'im exactly what I had done. I then searched every inch of the cabin, but no trace of the animal could be seen, an' the door was shut all the time. "Elp me!' says he, all of a shake. 'It's a warnin'. Somethin's goin' to 'appen to me.'"

"And did it?" asked one of the men.

"Yes. 'E married a woman who led him a fine old dance—used to chase 'im round the Dockyard wall and up Queen Street every time 'e went ashore, givin' 'im a piece of 'er mind."

"Is that all?" asked one of his listeners.

"Isn't that enough? I calls upon Ted Hinks to spin the next yarn."

"D'ye want to hear how I was disrated?" asked Hinks, knocking out his pipe and helping himself from another man's pouch. "Well, here it is: In '87, I was gunner's mate of the 'H——,' and a comfortable ship she was, except for one luff, a chap called Warmbath. One day while we were lying at Portland, this luff had charge of a party of men going to the rifle-range, and, as gunner's mate, I went too.

"The men marched in two companies in sections of fours, the lootenant and I being between the last file of the first company and the first section of the second company. Presently I saw the Commander coming down the hill towards us.'Here's the Commander coming, Mr. Warmbath,' says I. 'Make the men shoulder arms by companies as he passes'—for in those days it was shoulder, and not slope, arms.

"'Who told you to tell me my business, gunner's mate?' snapped old Warmbath, so I subsided like a thrashed cur; but I'm blowed if the luff didn't lose his head, for when the leading section came abreast the Commander he gave the order to 'present arms.'

"Some of the men actually obeyed the order and marched along with their rifles at the 'present,' like those wooden soldiers that kids play with; others sloped or shouldered arms, while the remainder simply carried on; but every man-jack of 'em laughed outright.

"'Mr. Warmbath, you'll report yourself to me on board,' was all the Commander said; but that was enough. When he got aboard he said it was all my fault—I had told him to make the men present arms. He was cautioned, I was disrated, and a precious long time it was afore I got made gunner's mate again.'"

"Couldn't you do anything in the matter?" I asked. "Surely the men nearest to you heard what you said to the lieutenant?"

"Yes, Mr. Reginald, they did," replied Hinks, "but there's no Court of Criminal Appeal in the Navy—at least, not yet."

"Now, Bill Stainer, it's your turn."

"Another time, mate; it's my watch below now."

Chapter XI

THE RED SEA

NINE days after leaving Gibraltar the "Fortuna" glided into the Grand Harbour at Malta, where, having obtained pratique*, we remained three days.*

Owing to the strong gales and head winds, another fourteen days passed ere we sighted the high light at Port Said, the northern entrance to the Suez Canal. Entering between two long and extremely low concrete breakwaters, we had to pay the necessary tolls and make a number of declarations before authority was given us to proceed. By the company's regulations we were compelled to make the passage through the Canal under power, and if unable to cover the entire length of eighty-seven miles by daylight, we should have to make fast by night, when, except under most urgent circumstances, no traffic is permitted.

It was noon, however, before the tedious journey commenced, and in consequence we had little hopes of arriving at Suez before nightfall.

The bos'n had overhauled the wire hawsers, and had cleared away one of the bow anchors, and had carried the kedge aft, so as to bring the yacht to a standstill in the event of a mishap. The awnings were rigged to mitigate the effects of the blazing sun, and a square of damp canvas was placed over the motor-case to prevent the gritty sand and dust from playing havoc with the engine.

The very monotony of the Canal made the hours drag slowly. Occasionally we passed a steamer, sometimes having to "tie up" to the bank to permit her to pass, but for the best part of the day there was nothing to be seen but a dreary bank of sand on either hand, and a long thread of sluggish water ahead. The heat, too, was terrific, and when, as frequently happened, a sudden squall swept down from the desert, the air was filled with particles of fine sand that made our eyes smart in a most painful manner.

One of these squalls occurred just as a large tramp steamer, high in ballast, was passing us. The "Fortuna," being protected to a certain extent by the bank, escaped with a shower of sand, but the steamer, her high sides offering an enormous surface to the blast, was blown broadside on to the lee shore, where she stopped dead against the bank, her propeller throwing up columns of sand and water till the engines could be stopped, and as long as she remained in sight we could see that the tramp was still aground.

A few miles farther we passed a "gare," or widening of the Canal, where two large vessels could pass, and barely had we gone another mile than there was an ominous dragging of the propeller. The man stationed at the motor immediately stopped the engine, and the anchor was let go. Something had fouled the propeller, and, reversing being futile, we were hung up in a helpless condition.

"It's a case, sir, I'm afraid," said the bos'n. "I think we had better tow her back to the siding and get help."

My father consented; the gig was lowered, and ten men rowed for the bank, paying out a stout hempen hawser as they went. Then, in the broiling sun, the party laid hold of the rope and marched slowly along the bank, their feet sinking deep in the loose, drifting sand.

It took over an hour to tow the "Fortuna" back to the gare, where we made fast and took steps to clear the propeller. Unwilling to unpack the diving-dresses, the bos'n got hold of some Arabs and explained to them in dumb show that something had fouled the propeller. Showing their white teeth in a broad grin that expressed that they had grasped the situation, two of the Arabs threw off their scanty clothing and dived beneath the yacht's counter.

For nearly a minute they remained beneath the surface, but, on reappearing, they made signs that a rope had wound itself round the screw; though, in spite of the bos'n's gesticulations, the Arabs refused to dive again, jabbering away in a language that was, of course, totally unintelligible to us.

At that moment a stout, big-built man, dressed in a blue surcoat and trousers and wearing a scarlet tarbouch, appeared on the scene, riding a small and miserably lean donkey and attended by two barefooted runners. Sliding awkwardly to the ground, he waddled to the edge of the Canal, and, addressing us in French, asked what had gone amiss.

The bos'n began to explain the situation, and at the same time the Arabs appealed to him; with the utmost capacity of their voices.

"It's one of the native officials of the Canal," explained the quartermaster, who had had previous experience of the East.

"Ask him to come aboard," said Uncle Herbert, and, stepping awkwardly into the gig, he was rowed alongside. Puffing and blowing like a grampus, he gained the deck, and after a few words with the Arabs he turned to my father.

"They want to be paid in advance," he explained in French, a language which the pater readily understood. "They are asking a hundred piastres (slightly over one pound) to clear the propeller, as they say the rope is wound round as hard as iron."

"Tell them that they will be paid directly they have finished the job," said my father resolutely, his Cornish determination beginning to assert itself, "or else I'll send our own divers down."

"Offer the old sinner five piastres for himself, sir," said the quartermaster in a stage aside. "He is not above taking baksheesh, I'll allow."

My father took the hint, and the Gippy jumped at the bait, for, seizing a stout stick which one of his attendants carried, he chased the Arabs over the side, belabouring and reviling them with all the energy at his command. This done, he waddled breathlessly to a deck-chair, and, seating himself, demanded the promised guerdon.

In the meantime four of the Arabs, armed with long knives, were working in relays, two at a time, and within half an hour the obstruction was removed and the propeller in working order.

Hardly had this task been completed and the men paid than the sun set, and with remarkable suddenness the daylight gave place to intense darkness, so the "Fortuna" was compelled to remain in the gare till sunrise.

The tropical heat of the day gave place to a piercing cold, a circumstance that surprised us, and we were glad to turn out our warm clothing, which, soon after leaving Gibraltar, we had discarded, as we had hoped, for months.

Just before turning in I went on deck, and, looking southwards, I noticed a glare in the sky. It turned out to be the searchlight of the P. and O. s.s. "Caledonia," which vessel, being privileged to proceed through the Canal at night, carries a powerful lamp that, with its operator, is suspended in a large cage over the bows.

Slowly the huge liner passed, leaving the darkness intensified by the blinding glare.

"A pretty sight, isn't if?" remarked my uncle, who had joined me on deck and was puffing at a cheroot.

"Rather!" I assented, drawing my coat collar over my ears. "But it's too chilly to stay here, so I think I'll turn in."

"Stay another ten minutes," he continued, pulling out his watch and peering at it by the glow of his cheroot, "and you'll see something that will well repay the trouble of waiting in the cold."

"Now," he added, after a few minutes' interval, "look over there"; and, following the direction of his outstretched arm, I saw nothing but the dim outlines of a break in the sand-hills that fringed the Canal.

Even as I looked, a dazzling red disc appeared to leap above the horizon, and in a moment the desert was flooded with a ruddy light. The moon had risen with all the splendour that is only met with in the rarefied atmosphere of tropic and sub-tropic climes.

In another quarter of an hour it was well above the horizon, bathing the surrounding country in a mellow light and casting long shadows of our spars athwart the opposite bank of the placid Canal.

"Splendid!" I exclaimed.

"Yes," assented my uncle, "and sunrise will be quite as rapid. Now go below and have a good night's rest, and I'm certain you won't turn out till we are nearly clear of this glorified ditch."

Uncle Herbert was right, for I did not awake till nearly noon, to find the cabin sweltering in the midday heat and the "Fortuna" passing through the last of the Bitter Lakes, Ismaïlia having been left astern two hours after daybreak.

A short stay at Suez, and the "Fortuna" cleared the southern entrance to the Canal, the town and the basins of Port Ibrahim being lost to view at a distance of three miles.

Before midnight we had emerged from the Gulf of Suez, catching but a short glimpse of the famous Mount Sinai against the western sky.

"You see that mountain just this side of it?" asked my uncle. "That's Jebel Katherina, more than a thousand feet higher and two miles to the west'ard of Sinai—yet almost every passenger on the Oriental liners firmly believes that he has seen the actual mountain mentioned in the Bible; but, as a matter of fact, this is the only position from which we can see it. In less than two minutes Sinai will be hidden by the other mountain. See, they are even now getting into line."

Next day we were in the centre of the Red Sea, keeping to the steamer routes to avoid possible encounters with Arab pirates, for, notwithstanding the complete occupation of Egypt and the Soudan, armed dhows still lurked in the little known harbours of the Arabian coast, and did not hesitate to attack and plunder any small craft likely to offer little or no resistance.

As a necessary precaution, and also for the purpose of exercising the crew in the use of small arms, the rifles were issued out, and seven rounds of ammunition were expended per man, the "Fortuna" being hove-to at a distance of six hundred yards from a floating barrel bearing a large red flag, while the officers observed and directed the firing through their field-glasses.

On the whole the results were remarkably good, taking into consideration the fact that most of the men had not handled a rifle for over a twelve-month.

Then, to the surprise of our crew, who were ignorant of its existence, the three-pounder quick firer was unpacked and mounted on the deck amidships, and the "Fortuna," taking up a position at a distance of a mile from the now waterlogged target, prepared to open fire.

Three men were detailed off as the gun's crew, and it was a sight to watch them as, stripped to their vests and trousers, they flew at the quick-firer, threw open the breech-block, and placed the long metal cylinder in the gun.

The gun-layer bent but for a few seconds over the sights, there was a flash and a sharp deafening report, followed by a slight haze of bluish vapour, and on looking through a telescope towards the target I was just in time to see the flag disappear in a column of spray.

"That's good enough for you, old stick, that is!" exclaimed the gun-layer approvingly, as he withdrew the cartridge-case, talking to the gun as if it were a child.

"Yes, you've done remarkably well, Hinks," remarked my father. "I don't think we need waste more ammunition."

"I pity any niggers that try to work off any of their little tricks on us, sir," replied the seaman, as the gun's crew began to clean the still smoking weapon.

The sight of the quick-firer and the small arms had, however, given rise to considerable speculation on the part of the crew, some hinting amongst themselves that, after all, the "Fortuna" might be intended for a pirate or slaver, and that they had been enticed to ship on board under false pretences. I overheard the quartermaster rating them, explaining that the armoury was simply and solely for defensive purposes, and this explanation apparently allayed the faint suspicions they had of the "Fortuna's" mission.

Soon after two bells in the first dog-watch (5 p.m.) on the second day after leaving Suez, my father called me on deck. Rapidly overhauling us was a large steamer flying the Turkish flag, her decks packed with a curious swarm of humanity. As she passed we could see, but not read, her name in Arabic characters on her stern.

"Lucky we are to windward, sir," remarked the bos'n, indicating the steamship with a contemptuous jerk of the thumb, "or we would nearly be driven below by the stench from her."

"Oh! How's that?"

"A pilgrim ship bound for Jidda, I'll allow. Half of 'em will be down with the plague unless they are particularly lucky."

"Wilkins is quite right in what he has just said," remarked Dr. Conolly, after the bos'n had made his way for'ard. "These ships, taking Mussulman pilgrims between Constantinople and Jidda, the nearest port to Mecca, the holy city of Mohammed, frequently have cases of bubonic plague on board, so that they are a standing menace to the health of Europe. Look! as it is they have left us a legacy."

In the wake of the Turkish ship were several huge sharks, two of which, in the hope of finding better food, devoted their attention to us, following the "Fortuna" at a distance of less than fifty yards.

Although only their black dorsal fins showed above the surface, the transparency of the water enabled the whole of their immense bodies to be distinctly seen. Along the Cornish coast at home, fish termed sharks by courtesy are frequently caught, and, although of the same family, having their mouths in the same position, they rarely exceed three feet in length; but these monsters were twelve or thirteen feet at the very lowest estimate.

"All right; carry on," replied my father to a request from the bos'n, and presently the crew were busily engaged in preparing a hook and line for their natural enemy.

Baiting the strong iron barb with a piece of red bunting, the line was carefully lowered over the taffrail. Directly it touched the water the sharks turned in evident alarm and disappeared, but after a few minutes a larger one swam cautiously towards the bait.

"Look out!—he'll have it!" shouted one of the crew in his excitement.

"Silence!" roared the bos'n, defeating his own object by the sound of his voice, for once more the shark turned and made off. His companion, however, approached the concealed hook, and, sinking beneath the surface, made ready to seize the bait, but, apparently scenting danger, he too sheered off.

"Try 'em with some pork," suggested Lord, the quartermaster, and accordingly Johnston brought us some fat pieces of salt meat, with which the hook was effectually concealed.

A few minutes' play with the new bait was sufficient. The larger shark reappeared, and, heedless of danger, headed straight for the prize. As it turned on its back; I could see its whitish yellow body, and the huge gaping jaws fringed with triple lines of serried teeth. There was a snap, and the stout rope tautened like an iron bar.

"Clap on, all of you!" yelled the bos'n to the men, but the order was unnecessary, as already the eager crew were hard at work; hauling in the line. When sufficient slack had been taken aboard, the free end was led outside everything to the fo'c'sle, and the men were ready to haul their prize on deck.

"Do you think we had better let them do it?" asked my father. "There is hardly room on deck for'ard, and besides, there will be such a filthy mess."

"Yes, let them work off their superfluous energies on it," replied my uncle. "An extra swabbing down of decks won't do much harm."

"Reggie," he added, "stay here and watch the fun, for a blow from a shark's tail can do a lot of damage, I can assure you."

At a word from the bos'n the men, who had armed themselves with axes and sheath-knives, began hauling again, and, in spite of its furious struggles, the monster was slowly but surely brought home, its powerful teeth snapping in impotent fury on the stout iron shank of the hook.

Then came an unexpected difficulty. The rope had been brought on board through a fairlead on the gunwale, and it was evident that no amount of strength could hoist the shark over the side, while with our fore and aft rig it was impossible to utilize the yards as derricks.

"Belay there!" shouted the bos'n, and, taking a few turns round the capstan, the crew stood easy and awaited orders. At a word from the bos'n one of the men swarmed up the fore-stay, taking with him a stropped block. This he bent to the stay at a distance of twenty-five feet from the deck, and, on going aloft the second time, the line was roved through the block and brought down on deck.

"Up with him, my hearties!" was the cry; and by the united efforts of ten of the crew the ponderous body of the shark came slowly over the side and dangled from the fore-stay, its tail slashing furiously in baffled rage.

At that moment, Johnston, the steward, hearing the outcry, appeared up the fore-hatch, holding a large tray of boiled potatoes in both hands. Suddenly, without warning, the strop of the block parted, and the shark fell with a thud on the narrow fo'c'sle. Instantly the men scattered right and left to escape the devastating sweeps of its tail and the huge snapping jaws; but before Johnston could disappear down the hatch a smashing blow of the creature's tail swept the dish of potatoes from his hand and smothered the ship's officers with a shower of sticky potato-meal!

But there was no time to enjoy the ludicrousness of the situation, and with excited shouts the men flew at their natural enemy, raining blows at its writhing carcass with hatchets and cudgels, till the decks were red with blood. At last, by a well-directed stroke, the creature's tail was severed, and the rest of the task became a comparatively easy matter.

Within a quarter of an hour the decks were swabbed down, the shark neatly skinned, and its jaw taken possession of by Dr. Conolly, as a remarkably fine specimen of the Carcharias vulgaris.

During the run down the Red Sea I had frequent opportunities of practising with my rifle on the numerous sharks that followed in the wake of the "Fortuna," and I rapidly became an expert marksman.

Aden was reached in due course; then, without any untoward incident, the "Fortuna" arrived at Point de Galle, in the Island of Ceylon, having been twenty-four days out from Suez.

Chapter XII

AT THE TREASURE ISLAND

AFTER a three days' stay at Point de Galle, during which time we shipped more stores and water, and replenished our oil-tanks with paraffin, the "Fortuna" headed east once more.

During our stay in port we had "signed-on" a new member of the crew, a tall and not bad-looking Arab, named Yadillah, who, by some means or the other, had been left at Ceylon from one of the mail-boats. He was engaged as cook and steward, thereby relieving Johnston of a task which was, in the tropical climates, none too pleasant. Yadillah could speak English fairly well, and, although he required special berthing and messing arrangements, he got on with the rest of the crew, in a most satisfactory manner.

In crossing the Bay of Bengal we caught the southern limit of the S.W. monsoon, so that, without having to requisition the motor, we made rapid progress as far as Singapore.

Thence navigation, mainly on account of the imperfect charting of these waters, became difficult; and as we approached the coral islands of the Pacific a man had to be constantly stationed at the cross-trees by day to look out for shoal water, while at night the "Fortuna" had to be kept under reduced sail, so as to bring-to at the first sign of danger.

Seven months had now elapsed since the day when the "Fortuna" cleared out from Fowey, and we were within a few hours' sail of the island where we hoped to find the "San Philipo" treasure. Every member of the crew was in a state of anxious tension, while my father and his brother, though outwardly calm, were in a fever of excitement. In spite of our sanguine hopes, there occurred the thought that possibly our reading of the cipher might be wrong, or that some one else might have forestalled us.

"Wind's falling light, sir," remarked the bos'n, as my father, in his impatience, had taken the third observation that morning.

"Yes, but with luck we'll make the island well before nightfall. Tell them to get the motor running."

Two hours sufficed to bring the jagged peaks of the Truk Archipelago above the horizon, and shortly afterwards, in fulfilment of my parent's forecast, the island known to us as the "San Philipo" hove in sight.

By my uncle's suggestion we headed away to starboard so as to approach the island in the same direction as did the fugitive "San Philipo" and her pursuer the "Anne," and, on drawing nearer, we saw that the island bore a strong resemblance to the description given by my roving ancestor.

There was the hill to the south-east, with its cat's-head outlines, and the two rugged headlands on the western side, and by the aid of a glass we could make out the mouth of a large cave, while all around the island, as far as we could see, was a long line of white foam, denoting the presence of the coral reef.

"Mast-head, there! Can you make out the entrance?" hailed my father.

"Aye, aye, sir—a point on the port bow."

"Then let her go," remarked the pater to the quartermaster. "We must get inside the reef before dark. Mr. Wilkins," he added, addressing the bos'n, "have the anchors cleared away, and keep the lead going."

"No bottom at twenty fathoms," reported the bos'n, after a few casts had been made.

Presently we on deck could distinguish a dark break in the turmoil of foaming water; it was the channel into the lagoon.

"Now or never!" exclaimed the quartermaster, who had relieved the man at the wheel, and was now steering straight for the gap. There was not a breath of wind, and had the "Fortuna" depended solely upon her sails we would have had to bring up till the breeze came, and with it, possibly a heavier sea on the reef.

"If the motor plays us false we are done for," remarked Uncle Herbert, who was anxiously regarding the smother of foam on either bow.

"Never fear; it has served us faithfully up to the present," replied my father. "Another five minutes will settle it."

Straight for the gap the "Fortuna" sped under full power, not a sound being heard above the loud roar of the breakers and the quick pulsations of the engine. On the crest of a huge wave she appeared to hang, then, plunging into the trough, her propeller raced, and her head fell off towards the reef. The spokes flew through the quartermaster's hands, and the staunch little yacht recovered herself, with tons of water pouring from her fo'c'sle. The next moment her stern sank deeply in the waves, the propeller gripped, and with a terrific lurch the "Fortuna" passed between the coral reefs and gained the shelter of the quiet lagoon. The anchor was let go, and, with a rush and a roar, the chain tore through the hawse-pipe, and the yacht brought up in six fathoms.

We had arrived at "San Philipo" Island.

Directly everything was snugged down, darkness had fallen on the scene, so that nothing further could be done that night. For the first time armed watches were set, but, though the sounds of paddles around the vessel and shouting on shore were heard at intervals, there was no attempt on the part of the natives to molest us.

At daybreak next morning we were awake, and on going on deck we could appreciate the natural beauty of our surroundings. The "Fortuna" lay directly over her anchor, which could be clearly seen on the sandy bottom. Not a ripple disturbed the placid surface of the lagoon, save an occasional gentle swell from the breakers on the reef, where day and night the huge green rollers lashed themselves in fury upon the coral rocks, churning themselves into milk-white foam to the accompaniment of a dull, subdued roar like the distant rumbling of an express train on a still night.

From where we lay the south-easternmost, or cat's-head, mountain was within a quarter of a mile, but only one of the western headlands was visible, as it effectually shut out its fellow. The cave that Humphrey Trevena had emphasized proved to be a huge rent in the cliff, made apparently by. volcanic action. Immediately in the centre of the southern side of the island—that is, the shore off which we lay—was a broad expanse of white sand, backed by a gently rising ground on which was a dense mass of vegetable growth, scrub and coco-nut palms being indiscriminately mingled. On the beach were half a dozen canoes, some, judging by their lofty prows and decorated sides, being used for war purposes; the others, being lighter and provided with out-riggers, were of the usual type used by the Pacific Islanders for fishing.

Around the canoes, and lining the shore, were hundreds of natives, who regarded the "Fortuna" with undisguised curiosity. By the aid of my telescope I could make them out very clearly. They were middle-sized, slender, and well-proportioned, though a few were of a stature that would be considered great even in Cornwall; their colour was almost that of the natives of the Malay Archipelago. Their features were small, but high and well-formed, their cheek-bones projecting, while both men and women had an abundance of glossy black hair. The majority were entirely naked, save for a conical covering for the head made of plaited and bleached leaves. In the foreground many of the men wore a kind of cuirass of stiff plaited cocoa-fibre, which was continued like half a stove-pipe to a distance of six inches above their heads. Their arms consisted of formidable swords with a jagged edge of sharks' teeth, and fearful-looking spears, terminating in a triple barb. A few, whom we took to be chiefs, wore in addition a complete covering of porcupine skin for the head, only their eyes being visible.

"A cheerful-looking set, aren't they?" remarked the doctor, who was also engaged in examining the throng of natives. "Do you think we are likely to have trouble with them?"

"The greatest tact will have to be employed if we wish to avoid a row," replied my father, with his eyes still glued to his field-glasses. "See, some of them are putting off in their canoes."

Already they had launched two of their largest craft, while knots of natives were busily engaged in hauling down the rest.

"Serve out the small arms, Mr. Lord, please," said my father; "but take care that we give no sign likely to provoke a fight. Herbert, will you see to the quick-firer and the Maxim."

Quickly, yet quietly, our preparations for defence were made. The three-pounder was placed on its mounting amidships, which had not been removed since the gunnery practice in the Red Sea, and the Maxim, concealed behind a square of canvas, was mounted on its tripod so as to command the water between us and the shore, while each man placed his rifle, with charged magazine, on the deck within hand's reach.

Hardly was this done than the natives' flotilla came within hailing distance. The warriors, decked in their barbaric finery, were grouped in the prow of their war canoes. Many of them bore livid scars, the legacy of many a tribal fight, and in their panoply a more repulsive and savage crowd I never wish to see. In that moment of actual danger I felt a peculiar trembling of the limbs and dry sensation in my throat. From the canoes I turned my eyes towards my companions. The crew seemed perfectly cool and determined, a circumstance that somewhat reassured me. Dr. Conolly was evidently labouring under strong physical excitement, as if anxious to begin the fray, while my father, though in no doubt as to the issue, was evidently reluctant to give the order to open fire on the yelling crowd of savages, who, brandishing their swords and spears, had drawn up within fifty yards, the paddles of their canoes resting motionless on the water.

"Cannot we let rip at the vicious brutes?" asked the doctor. "They will be over the side in a minute if we don't."

"Not if it can possibly be helped," replied my father. "Where's Herbert?" he added hurriedly.

There was no sign of my uncle on deck, but, on being called, he replied, from below, "Wait half a second."

Standing on the rail, my father held up a piece of brilliantly dyed cloth and a string of gaudy glass beads as a peace-offering to the aggressive natives, but the only reply was a shower of stones, hurled from slings of cocoa-cloth, that whizzed over our heads. It was only by quick descent that my father missed the unwelcome present.

"Lie down, men!" he shouted, "and stand by with your arms!"

Another volley of stones came from the natives, some striking the ship's side, others humming through the rigging. As I lay flat on the deck I saw a huge copper helmet emerge from the companion hatchway, and Uncle Herbert, dressed in a diver's suit, without, of course, the air tubes and lead sinkers, came on deck.

Striding to the side, he faced the warlike mob, and instantly, to the accompaniment of a chorus of "Ohe! Owha!" the natives took up their paddles and made for the shore.

"That's done it," laughed Uncle Herbert, removing the copper head-dress, which was rendering its wearer most uncomfortably hot, even in the slanting rays of the early morning sun.

"Stop, you idiot!" exclaimed my father, laying a detaining hand on his brother's shoulders; but the warning was too late. Some of the natives in the hindermost canoe saw the helmet being removed, and, calling to their fellows, the whole of the boats turned and made for the yacht.

"We are in for it this time!" exclaimed Dr. Conolly. "See, they are making for both sides at once."

Such was the case. Two war canoes and five smaller ones (where they had come from I do not know) made for the starboard side, and the remaining war canoes, with three others, headed for the port side.

"Money," exclaimed my father to the man in charge of the quick-firer, indicating the largest craft that was making obliquely across our bows, "can you manage to put a shot through that fellow's bow?"

"Aye, aye, sir, I'll try."

Calmly, yet deliberately, the gun's crew opened the breech-block and thrust home the gleaming cylinder with its deadly head. Hardly had the breech-block been replaced than Money hung on the sights for a brief second. There was a flash and a roar, and the next moment the shot tore a gaping hole in the stem of the canoe, and, after a series of ricochets, struck the cliff with terrific force, bringing down large masses of rock. The stricken craft immediately became waterlogged, its occupants, all swimmers from their infancy, striking out vigorously for the shore, while the remainder of the boats turned tail in a panic.

"Lower away the whaler and pick up as many as you can," shouted my father, and, in obedience to the order, the men sprang to the falls. The boat had fortunately been already cleared away, so that it was the work of a few moments to lower it.

In spite of their frantic struggles, five of the natives were picked up, tied hand and foot, and brought back to the yacht, where, surrounded by the crew, they were placed on the deck.

"Now for a little moral persuasion," exclaimed my father, and, looking round, he noticed a small grove of coco-palms growing close to the water's edge at a distance of about a quarter of a mile.

"Show them a charge, Money," he continued; "then plank a shot right into the centre of those trees."

The gunner exhibited the projectile, a common shell, to the terrified savages; then, in full view, he placed the charge in the gun.

"Ready, sir!" he announced.

In obedience to an order, the natives were raised to their feet and made to look in the direction of the grove. Once more the quick-firer barked, and the highly charged projectile, bursting in the centre of the group of trees, levelled four of them in a shower of splinters and a dense cloud of smoke, while the savages, in their fright, sank to the deck and uttered shrill cries of terror.

"Cut that man loose," continued my father, indicating one of the captives, who, by reason of the loss of their fantastic war paint and finery, were by no means unintelligent in appearance.

Offers of presents were unavailing, the man refusing to look at the glittering baubles that were shown him. Some one suggested giving him a plug of tobacco, but, though the offer had a strong attraction, the native still remained in sullen isolation.

"Perhaps he thinks we are going to eat him," suggested the doctor.

"Let me 'ave a rub at him, sir," exclaimed Mills, one of the deck hands.

"Have a what?" asked Dr. Conolly.

"A rub at 'im. Rubbin' noses is what they does in these 'ere parts as a sign of affection like."

"By all means," replied the doctor, laughing; "I don't suppose Captain Trevena has any objection."

Without further ado, Mills took hold of the native's shoulders, and, thrusting his face forward, he applied his nasal organ to that of the savage, and, as if by magic, the latter's taciturn manner completely vanished. The remaining four prisoners were then cut loose and subjected to the same ceremony, and, on being given a ship's biscuit apiece, they squatted on the deck, stuffing the food down their throats, and chattering in a lively, yet absolutely indistinguishable, fashion.

At length, laden with the pieces of coloured cloth and glass beads which, in their fright, they had previously refused, the natives were taken ashore in the whaler, and, after exaggerated gestures of goodwill, they vanished into the woods.

"That's satisfactory so far," commented my parent on the return of the boat; "but we must be very careful to guard against treachery. Pipe all hands to breakfast, Mr. Wilkins, and then we'll set about to find the remains of the 'San Philipo.'"

Chapter XIII

WE FIND THE WRECK

THE day was well advanced before the preparations for the finding of the wreck were completed, and the blazing sun beat down with terrific heat upon the surface of the glassy sea. Both boats were lowered, and tropical awnings rigged to protect their crews, who, clad in the lightest of white clothing and wearing straw hats, were full of enthusiasm for work in spite of the enervating heat.

In the whaler went my father, the doctor, and five seamen, while the gig contained Uncle Herbert, three seamen, and myself; the bos'n and the quartermaster, two deck hands, and Yadillah remaining on board the "Fortuna." Both boats were armed, while the Q.-F. was ready for instant action in case of a surprise.

A gentle pull for about half a mile brought the boats to the approximate position of the wreck of the Spanish treasure ship. This we found to be just inside the reef, which at this point was less than a foot above the surface, the gush of the breakers causing a heavy swell as the larger of the rollers broke over the ridge of coral.

Inside the reef at this point the lagoon was too deep to distinguish the bottom, while, judging from the colour of the water, it descended abruptly into a large hole or crater. After sounding for two hours we found that such was the case, for, although the average depth of the lagoon was but six fathoms, there was a sunken bed, roughly 400 yards in length and 120 in breadth, where bottom was found at from twelve to fifteen fathoms, the deepest part being close to the reef. By the "arming" of the lead—the tallow placed in a cavity in the bottom of the sinker—the bed was found to be composed, not of fine white sand like the greater part of the lagoon, but of mud and sand mixed into a dark, gritty substance, with plenty of vegetable growth.

It was the time of spring tides, and the rise, though but three feet, was sufficient to prevent the divers from descending on account of the constant swell over the reef; so, while waiting till the tide had subsided sufficiently to allow the coral to act as a breakwater, the grapnels were brought into play in the hope of finding some portions of the wreck.

Cast after cast resulted in nothing more than the disturbing of the bottom to such an extent that the clear water became discoloured till it resembled liquid mud, and though masses of long, tendril-like seaweed were brought up, there were no indications of any foreign substance lying on the floor of the lagoon. At length one of the irons brought up a piece of wood, water-logged and covered with weeds and barnacles.

Whipping out his knife, Uncle Herbert scraped the excrescences from the piece of timber and, to the delight of the crews of both boats—for the whaler, on hearing of the find, had come alongside the gig—he announced that it was a fragment of oak planking, with the marks of the bolts and trenails still plainly visible.

"It's part of an old ship, beyond doubt," he remarked. "See! the wood is almost as hard as iron, yet black with years of submersion in salt water. I think we are somewhere near the mark."

"So far, so good," replied my father. "But I think we'll have a spell now. Just buoy the spot before we leave, and the divers can descend later in the day."

We returned to the "Fortuna," the boats being left at the booms instead of being hoisted inboard, while the diving-suits were carefully overhauled and the valves tested.

While we were at lunch the bos'n reported: "Natives coming off, sir."

"Bother the natives!" exclaimed Dr. Conolly. "Their attentions are becoming too frequent. Let's see what they want this time."

Upon going on deck we found that a fleet of twenty small outrigger canoes was approaching, their occupants being without the war costumes which they wore on the previous occasion. As they came nearer they waved their hands in token of friendship, and displayed baskets of yams, coconuts, taro, and bananas, while one or two had live pigs trussed to bamboos.

"We shall have to watch them carefully," remarked my father, "although they are not armed. Keep your rifles handy, but on no account frighten them. The provisions will be most acceptable, for we will have to be dependent on the island for food and water for some time."

The leading canoe came dexterously alongside, and a tall, well-built man, who was apparently a chief, sprang up the side and gained the deck, accompanied by five of his companions. Others would have followed, but by a peremptory gesture the bos'n kept them off.

The chief, who was head and shoulders taller than the rest of the natives, ran towards my father and went through the nose-rubbing ceremony, doing the same honour to my Uncle Herbert, Dr. Conolly, and myself; then, rapidly speaking a few words to his companions, he made signs for us to accept the presents they brought.

In a few minutes the various eatables were flying over the bulwarks in a manner somewhat resembling, but far more pleasant than, the shower of stones with which they had greeted us on the previous day, till the skylight was heaped with enough fruit and vegetables to last us a week, and half a dozen squealing pigs lay struggling in the scuppers.

In return we presented the chief with a small looking-glass, which he hung round his neck, a hatchet, some cloth and beads, and two empty three-pounder brass cylinders. The latter he received with considerable trepidity, but finally he bound them with a strip of cocoa-fibre and dangled them from his mop of thick hair, laughing in high glee as they clanked with every movement of his head.

We then took him all over the yacht, keeping a sharp eye on the natives, who, having recovered their usual spirits, were laughing and talking and making signs in dumb show like delighted children, and showed a tendency to pilfer any small metal articles they could conveniently hide. Even when detected in the act of thieving they would roar with merriment as if proud of being found out, and on putting down the stolen articles they would rub noses with the nearest member of the crew, and immediately lay hands on the next object that took their fancy.

For the chief's edification the Q.-F. was discharged, upon which he fell on the deck and hid his head in his arms. To still further impress him, a barrel was towed to a good distance from the yacht and a few rounds from the maxim knocked it into a multitude of splinters. The bilgepump took his fancy to such an extent that he ordered two of his followers to continue working on it, till the pump sucked dry with a gurgling noise that caused the men to drop the levers as if they were red-hot.

At length, after many signs whereby he clearly expressed a wish for us to visit him ashore, the chief was induced to go over the side, and to the accompaniment of a weird song of welcome uttered by fifty lusty voices, he was paddled at a great rate to the beach.

"A spell ashore will be a change, Reggie," remarked my father. "Shall we have a look at their village?"

"Will it be safe?"

"I think so, if we take proper precautions. The natives evidently have had a good object-lesson, and I don't think they will give us any trouble."

So the gig was manned, and my father, the doctor, myself, and five men went ashore. We were all armed, and, in addition, four large breakers were taken in order to replenish the supply of fresh water.

"We will be back within two hours, I hope," said my father to Uncle Herbert on pushing off; "keep an eye on the shore, however, although I don't anticipate any trouble. In the meantime get the diving-gear into the whaler and we'll make a start directly we return."

Nearly the whole village awaited us on the sandy shore, and once again the ceremony of rubbing noses was performed with the chief and several of the head men. Leaving two of the men to guard the boat, with instructions to lie a few yards off shore and to fire their rifles should they hear the report of ours, we made our way towards the village, accompanied by the chief men and followed by the shouting throng.

There was a broad but winding path through the dense scrub, which, ascending a gentle rise, presently entered a thick belt of palm-trees. On one side of the road was a bubbling stream, but from the "Fortuna" there were no signs of its entering the sea, so we concluded it fed a lake in the depths of the brushwood.

On emerging from the palm-wood half an hour later we came upon a large clearing, in the centre of which was a stockade surrounding the village. A narrow gateway gave access to the huts, which were substantially built and roofed with palm-leaves. The chief led the way to his house, a long structure built of trimmed trunks of trees, decorated in many vivid colours.

Outside was a kind of veranda, under which rugs of coco-fibre were placed, and squatting down on his heels, the chief motioned us to do likewise, while pieces of baked meat, yams, and coco-nuts were placed before us.

"I don't think we had better touch the meat," remarked the doctor. "It might be——" and a suggestive shrug of his shoulders completed the sentence.

"Do you think it possible that these men are cannibals?" I asked.

"Possible and highly probable," replied Dr. Conolly. "But that we shall soon find out."

Presently the chief clapped his hands, and the crowd in front of us, who were regarding us with the greatest curiosity, fell back, forming a large semicircle. Into the space sprang two men, dressed in full native armour of thick fibre with fish-skin helmets, and without a moment's hesitation they attacked each other with large clubs of heavy wood.

Yelling and shouting, they jumped about with marvellous agility, their ponderous weapons clashing with a dull thud so frequently that the sound resembled the beating of a rattle.

"Don't worry, Reggie," said my father, noticing the anxious look on my face; "they are only playing to amuse us—a sort of return on the part of the chief for showing him——"

"Are they playing? Look!" exclaimed the doctor, springing to his feet, for at that moment one of the combatants, nimbly avoiding a sweeping blow, had shortened his club and struck his opponent fairly between the eyes. The fish-skin crumpled before the blow as if made of paper, and the man sank senseless to the ground, and with a whoop of triumph the victor tore off the other's head-dress, and, drawing a jagged-edged sword of shark's teeth, proceeded to make a variety of fancy cuts and passes before hewing off the head of his senseless victim.

"Stop that!" shouted the doctor, in a voice that made his meaning perfectly clear, and, seeing that the savage was still bent on carrying out his intention, Dr. Conolly sprang over the intervening ground in three bounds, and, before the man could grasp the situation, he struck him such a blow on the extremity of the jaw-bone that, in spite of the protection afforded by the stiff cocoafibre, the native was hurled backwards as if struck by a thunderbolt.

Fortunately for us, the chief took this interruption in apparent good part; the stricken victor of the fight picked himself up and disappeared amongst the crowd while the senseless man was carried to a hut in a most indifferent manner by a party of women.

Presently my father made signs to the chief that he would like to inspect the village, to which request he assented.

Facing the chief's hut was a stockade similar to, though smaller than, that which surrounded the village, and towards this he led the way. At the gateway were two men, dressed in long cloak-like dresses of white feathers, their faces painted red and yellow, and their hair stiffened out like an enormous turban. Bending thrice, the chief made obeisance to these fearsome-looking individuals, then he turned and walked slowly past the gate, without attempting to enter.

"What's inside, I wonder?" exclaimed the doctor. "Let's have a peep in." And, leaving us, he made for the entrance to the inner stockade; but, before he could carry out his intention, the crowds of natives who followed in our footsteps ran between him and the gate, uttering shrill cries of rage, while the chief, roused to sudden anger, seized him by the shoulders and dragged him away, as if incensed at the doctor's audacity.

It seemed as if a serious affray was imminent, but at length the tumult died away, and the chief resumed his tour of inspection, though, I noticed, he scowled at Dr. Conolly whenever he glanced that way.

"They cut up pretty rough over that affair, didn't they?" remarked the doctor, on returning to the shore.

"Yes; I thought we were in for trouble. You really must be careful, Conolly, not to offend them."

"But I couldn't sit there and see a fellow's head hacked off in that cold-blooded fashion."

"I do not refer to that, although the consequences might have been awkward. It's the other incident. No doubt that enclosure contains a temple, and is held in veneration by these savages."

"They are only a horde of heathen fanatics."

"Yes, but there are quite enough of them to wipe us out. Remember, we are not here to give the British Government an excuse for colonial expansion, but to try and wrest a treasure from the depths of the ocean.

However, here come the men with the breakers, so we'll hurry back to the yacht."

The fresh-water barricoes were placed in the gig, and we shoved off, the boat cutting through the placid water at a great pace, for much work had to be done in the three hours that remained before sunset.

On running alongside the "Fortuna" the breakers were slung on board, and, in company with the whaler, in which were the divers and their apparatus, we made for the buoy marking the spot where the piece of timber had been brought up by the grapnel.

Here the whaler was anchored fore and aft, and the two divers, Lewis and Burbidge, who were already clad in their dresses, were taken in hand by their attendants, who proceeded to affix the lead weights to their shoes, back, and chest. Then the copper helmets were firmly secured, the life-line and air-tube connections made, and the glass front was screwed in position.

The air-pumps began to work, and, assisted by willing hands, both divers crawled over the side of the whaler, and amidst a turmoil of bubbles caused by the escaping air, they sank beneath the surface. For a considerable distance they were plainly visible, but gradually their grotesque outlines grew fainter and fainter, till a slight bubbling on the surface alone betrayed their whereabouts.

Over half an hour passed, but no signal came from either man, though we observed that the water became discoloured with dirt, and the train of bubbles, after leading some distance from the boats, finally became stationary. The divers had ceased their submarine walk, and had evidently found something worthy of their attention.

At length came a series of tugs on the life-lines, and slowly ropes and air-tubes came home over the gunwale, till both copper helmets appeared simultaneously on opposite sides of the whaler, where ready hands helped the wearers on board.

"Found anything?" asked my father, the moment the glass discs were unscrewed.

"Yes, sir," replied Lewis, who held in his hand a weed-grown object that had once been a dead-eye. "Yes, sir. She's there, right enough, but she's sunk in the mud and sand, and her decks are covered with long weeds ."

"Aye," assented Burbidge. "She's on an even keel, but nearly flush with the bottom; and, worse luck, her decks seem as sound as ever they were."

"Not worse luck," replied my father "for had the decks been rotten, the timbers would have been rotten also, and the wreck would have been strewn all over the bed of the lagoon. All we have to do, my lads, is to put a charge under her upper deck and blow it up."

"And then?" asked the doctor.

"And then," rejoined my father, with a voice that carried conviction, "we'll bring up the treasure."

Chapter XIV

A TERRIBLE ORDEAL

FOR the next four or five days the work on the hull of the ill-fated "San Philipo" proceeded apace; for, as the announcement had been made that all hands would be entitled to a share in the proceeds, the crew loyally assisted in the operations, working long hours, in spite of the terrific heat, to bring about the ultimate success of the undertaking.

The natives of the island were very attentive in their visits, and they gave no signs of animosity, but, on the contrary, seemed more like curious children than the savages who had attempted to board the "Fortuna." Although we bore in mind the warning given in nautical works against the treachery of the inhabitants of these islands, we came to the conclusion that these were too thoroughly overawed by our armed strength to attempt to molest us further; so excursions were frequently made on shore without observing any cause or symptoms of aggression. Nevertheless, none of us ever set foot on the island without being armed.

"The watering party are going ashore this afternoon," remarked Dr. Conolly to me on the fifth day after our arrival off the island. "I think I'll have a run up to the village. Would you like to come with me?"

"Rather!" I replied enthusiastically.

"Then ask your father if he has any objection."

"By all means go," replied the pater, when I mentioned the matter; "but, mind you, no skylarking. Take your sporting rifle with you, but on no account shoot at anything, for the natives have peculiar notions, regarding certain animals with almost religious veneration; and should you shoot one of their pet pigs—almost the only animals on these islands—you may bring the whole tribe of savages about your ears."

So that afternoon we went ashore, and, leaving the men with the water-breakers, the doctor and I, accompanied by Yadillah, made our way towards the village, followed, as usual, by a throng of curious natives.

As we passed through the coco-nut grove swarms of pigs and fowls crossed our path, while overhead we saw numerous brilliantly feathered birds, which, curiously enough, were songless. Presently we came to the part of the road where the little stream babbled by the side of the path.

"I wonder where that brook runs to," remarked Dr. Conolly, glancing towards the thicket into which it plunged. "I don't remember seeing the spot where it joins the sea."

"It will be a hard matter to follow it," I replied, pointing to the dense clusters of prickly shrub that formed a formidable barrier over its course. "But surely it must reach the sea somewhere."

"Not necessarily; but, if it does, its outlet must be on the shore off which the 'Fortuna' is lying, otherwise it must defy the laws of gravity and climb the hill on our right. My impression is, however, that it falls into a vast chasm, and the basaltic nature of the rocks strengthens my conviction."

"That sounds interesting."

"It does. As the island is composed largely of basalt, and shows signs of volcanic action, there can be no doubt as to its origin. Thousands of years ago a mighty earthquake must have shot this and hundreds of other islands above the surface, and from the floor of the vast submarine plateau the coral builders are doing their work of making new ground."

"Shall we try to trace the course of this stream, then? Yadillah has a large knife, so that we can clear a path through the scrub."

"Well, there's no harm in attempting it. Yadillah, you black imp!"

"Yas, sahib."

"Cut a path for us through this stuff." The Arab attacked the undergrowth vigorously, and, working as he went, disappeared in the tunnel that he had cut above the stream. Presently he returned with the information that the thicket extended only a short way, and that the brook ran through a dense coco-nut grove.

"Lead on, then, Yadillah," exclaimed the doctor. "You follow, Reggie, and I'll bring up the rear."

"Clear off, you niggers," he added, speaking authoritatively to the natives, who were regarding our movements with ill-concealed excitement. The doctor's words and actions had the desired effect, for the crowd of followers stood back, jabbering incessantly, save a few who made off towards the village.

Although we kept our thick water-tight boots on, the water was deliciously cool as we waded down the stream, bending low to escape the rough tendrils that overhung the low tunnel that the Arab had cut for us. A few steps brought us to the other side of the vegetable barrier, and, as Yadillah had said, the brook flowed through a fairly dense palm-grove, its bed being composed of hard, slippery rock.

After we had proceeded a few hundred yards the doctor suddenly exclaimed—

"Hullo! This looks interesting. There's a well-worn path here. I suppose it leads to the village."

"But why interesting?"

"For one reason, there is no actual necessity for the natives to make a well-worn path to the brook, as plenty of water can be had in the village; for another, I think we have stumbled on some secret place where these savages hold their religious ceremonies. I am not sure, mind you, but the circumstances point that way."

The path descended abruptly into what appeared to be a vast circular hollow, though the dense clusters of trees and bushes prevented us from seeing the opposite side of the rock-bound circle. The stream now became a rushing torrent, leaping from rock to rock in a series of spray-fringed cascades, and the only sound that broke the silence of the spot was the noise of the falling water.

"This must have been the crater of an active volcano at one time," said the doctor in a low tone, as if influenced by the solitude of the spot. "I think we'll find I am right about the outlet of the stream."

At length we reached the bottom of the vast cavity, and in the unaccustomed twilight caused by the foliage and the overhanging rocks (though it was still broad daylight) we could see a large pool of dark water, and, surrounding this lakelet, were a number of posts, each about six feet in height, and most of them were surmounted by a grinning skull, while a fetid atmosphere hung over the place like a pall.

I felt the colour leave my face at the horror of the sight, and, glancing at the doctor, I noticed that his jaw was firmly set and his eyebrows knitted in grim determination. Yadillah, though used to scenes of cruelty in his younger days, turned an ashy grey, and I heard him mutter a sentence in which the word "Allah" caught my ear.

"What does it mean?" I whispered.

"They are the skulls of men killed in tribal fights, to take the mildest view of the situation," replied Dr. Conolly. "But I should not be surprised if this is the scene of gruesome practices of cannibalism."

"Come on, let's get away from this horrible place," I exclaimed.

"One moment," he replied, and, picking up a piece of stone, he threw it into the pool, which, although it obviously was fed by the stream, was absolutely unruffled on its surface.

The ripples caused by the stone had barely reached the edge of the pond when a loathsome head appeared above the water and a pair of lidless eyes stared malignantly at us. Then, with an eel-like motion, the monster began to swim towards the spot where we were standing. It was a gigantic water-snake.

"Ugh, you brute!" shouted the doctor, and, regardless of the consequences, he drew his Webley revolver and sent a .441-in. bullet crashing through the monster's head. With a quick motion the reptile turned and disappeared beneath the surface, discolouring the dark water with its blood; but hardly had the echoes of the report died away when the surrounding brushwood seemed alive with men, who, uttering furious cries, made directly for us.

The surprise was complete, for before the doctor could raise his weapon or the rest of us lift a hand in self-defence we were borne to the ground and bound hand and foot with ropes of coco-fibre.

The next few moments seemed like a dream. I was dimly conscious of the horde of yelling, savages, who danced around and over our prostrate bodies with every attitude of demoniac fury. Three of their number, evidently priests, judging by their fantastic garb and the bizarre markings of red and white paint that concealed their faces, stood by the edge of the pool solemnly calling upon their outraged deity; but whether the brute was dead or only wounded I could not ascertain, for their efforts were in vain.

At one time it seemed as if the natives would have thrown us into the gruesome pool, but after a great deal of excited jabbering they eventually lashed each of us to a long bamboo and, carried between two men, we were taken towards the village, the shouting natives following in a disorderly mob.

The path led to a gateway other than the one by which we had entered a few days previously, but we were carried to the open space in front of the chief's house. It was a very different reception from our last visit that now awaited us, for the chief, after receiving a report from the priests, stepped over to where the doctor was lying and placed his foot on his neck. He then addressed the crowd, and at the conclusion of his speech a mighty shout went up, and, lifted shoulder high, we were borne into the inner stockade, the same which Dr. Conolly had tried to investigate, and were placed side by side on a low wicker bench.

Though tightly bound to the bamboo pole, I could move my head slightly—just enough, in fact, to see my companions. I was lying between them. The doctor was writhing ineffectually in his bonds, his face red with the exertion; Yadillah's features were absolutely impassive, the Asiatic fatalism having supreme mastery over any emotion under which he might be labouring.

We were alone, for the priests and the crowd of natives were without the gates, making the place ring with their blood-curdling shouts.

At last by a great effort I raised my head sufficiently to look before me, and facing us was a huge wooden image, bedaubed with paint and feathers, while in front was a row of skulls painted a vivid red and an immense block of polished stone. What was behind me I could not observe, but I knew that there was a fire burning within a few yards of where we were lying.

"Reggie," said the doctor in a low tone that I hardly recognized, "I am afraid we are done for. It's all my fault."

"What's going to happen?" I asked fearfully.

"I cannot say," he replied. "But unless we are rescued I doubt whether we'll see to-morrow's sun. Idiot that I was to let fly at that pond brute!"

"Do you think they heard the shot on board the 'Fortuna'? If so, they'll think something is wrong and will send a search-party to look for us."

"The distance was too great, and we were in a deep hollow. Our only chance is that they will search for us when we do not return by sunset. Are you hurt?"

"No, only stiff. Are you?"

"My neck is pretty sore where that brute of a chief trod on it. I should dearly like to have the chance of settling with him. Ah! here they come again!"

Five or six of the savages approached, bringing with them another bound prisoner, a native, whom they placed next to Yadillah. Then, unlashing us from the bamboos, they cut away most of our clothing and lashed us to the block of stone in front of the idol, our arms being extended above our heads in an excruciating position.

The native prisoner was on my extreme left, Yadillah between him and me, and Dr. Conolly on the right. The priests then bent over the native and did something which caused him to groan dismally. They did the same to the Arab, but not a sound came from his lips; then it was my turn. I could not see what they were doing, but in my imagination I felt the sharp point of a knife against my bare chest, and I could hardly forbear from shrieking aloud. However, I still lived, and by craning my neck I saw that the priests were painting a black spot surrounded by a white circle on the doctor's ribs immediately over his heart. Whatever it meant, we had all been treated in the same way; but the fact of being fastened to what was undoubtedly an altar-stone told me that we were to be sacrificed to the grinning idol.

At length the sun set, and the short tropical twilight gave place to intense darkness. The village was as silent as the tomb, and, stretched upon that awful bed, my ears were intently listening for the faintest sound, while my eyes tried to discern the grim outlines of the idol, expecting every moment to be my last.

Suddenly above the distant palm-covered hills the disc of the full moon appeared, and instantly the air was filled with the shouts of the savages, who, beating drums and clapping their hands, poured in through the gate of the inner stockade in a compact body, till the courtyard of the temple was filled to overflowing.

The bright lunar beams cast the shadow of the idol slightly in front of our feet, but the priests, using some rough mechanical device, thrust the terrible image forward so that its shade, as the moon rose higher, would inevitably fall athwart our bodies. Into the monster's outstretched hand was placed a long brass-hilted sword, which overhung us in a menacing manner.

The shouting ceased as if by magic, and the priests with much ceremony killed three fowls, holding their bodies towards the moon and afterwards sprinkling the idol with their blood. Then, holding the doctor's revolver in a suppliant attitude, one of the savage officiates presented it to the idol; but as he did so he must have touched the trigger, for the weapon exploded, sending a bullet through the priest's arm and bringing down one of the natives in the crowd of worshippers. Superstitious awe fell upon the multitude; but with marvellous self-control the wounded priest picked up the revolver and, regardless of his arm, which hung helpless at his side, placed it at the feet of the idol.

In absolute silence the worshippers looked towards the priests, who in turn were eagerly regarding the upward path of the satellite.

During that awful time I lay in a sort of stupor, realizing my danger, yet filled with a complete indifference as to my fate. I was dimly conscious of the grinning idol, the fiendish painted faces of the priests, and the shouts of the crowd, which sounded like the subdued roar of a number of wild beasts; but the whole time my thoughts were fixed upon my home in peaceful Cornwall, and the various trifling incidents of my life flashed in quick succession through my brain.

The priests, one holding the knife in his uplifted hand, again watched the progress of the fateful shadow as it slowly climbed the Arab's side and approached his bare chest. In a firm voice the Moslem made the declaration of his faith: "Walla ghalib illah Allah!" he cried defiantly, and awaited the fatal stroke.

But it never came. The priest gave a hasty glance towards the moon, then, with a yell of superstitious terror, he dropped the knife and ran screeching through the crowd. The other priests followed his example, the panic became general, and in less than a minute the temple was deserted, save by the bound but living men, while from the village came the terrified wailings of the demoralized savages.

I spoke to the doctor, my voice broken and feeble, but no reply came from his lips; then I turned my head towards the Arab, who was vigorously but ineffectually struggling with his bonds, and he, too, had his eyes fixed on the moon.

My torpor had passed, and now I was eager to see the cause of this sudden diversion in our favour, and, following the direction of Yadillah's glance, I saw a dark shadow slowly creeping over the surface of the moon, and already its light was waning.

It was an eclipse; the penumbra had extended over half the satellite's hemisphere, and the umbra was rapidly following. To the ignorant savages the phenomenon could have but one meaning. They had offered sacrifices to the goddess of the night, and the goddess by hiding her face had scorned them, and dire calamity was bound to follow this mark of rejection.

How long I lay on that stone of sacrifice I cannot tell, but throughout the whole of the total eclipse, when everything was as dark as the blackest night and nature was hushed into absolute silence, I was fully awake to the possibilities of rescue or death. At length the umbra began to pass slowly across the moon, and a dim, greyish light faintly played on the grim outlines of the temple. In another two hours it would be daylight, and the savages would return and hale us to our deaths.

But presently I heard the sound of footsteps, not the light tread of the barefooted savage, but the tramp of booted men, and lusty voices shouted our names. We were saved!

"This way! Here, in the temple!" I cried as loud as my exhausted strength would permit; and as the crew of the "Fortuna," headed by my father, rushed into the stockade my senses left me, and I fell into a deep swoon.

Chapter XV

THE DEFENCE OF THE TEMPLE

WHEN I recovered my senses the sun had risen above the horizon, and I found myself lying within the stockade of the temple—not in the clutches of the bloodthirsty savages, but surrounded by my friends. Yet without the wooden fence were the natives, who, judging by their shrill cries and shouts of defiance, had recovered from their superstitious panic. I sat up and looked wearily around.

The idol, with its outstretched sword, doubtless a relic from a castaway Spanish warship, still remained as if to dispel any thoughts that the previous night had been but a horrible dream; there was the stone of sacrifice, and two smouldering heaps of charred wood still marked the spot where the fires for the interrupted cannibal feast had been lighted.

The stockade had been hastily adapted for purposes of defence. The Maxim, on its light tripod, commanded the open square without the gate, and around it was a group of seamen, to whom my father was giving various orders.

Uncle Herbert, with the rest of the men—for the whole of the "Fortuna's" crew save two, who were left on board, had taken part in the brave attempt at rescue—was busily engaged in loopholing the stockade at convenient distances, while Dr. Conolly, who had apparently completely recovered from his terrible ordeal, had regained possession of his revolver and was overhauling its mechanism. Yadillah still preserved his impassive demeanour, but into the folds of his voluptuous girdle, which he had recovered in a practically unsoiled state, he had thrust a long knife and a heavy Service revolver.

"Hello, Reggie!" exclaimed my father, who, seeing me slowly arise, had left the party with the Maxim and had hastened over to where I was sitting. "Feeling better, eh? Well, pull yourself together, and give a hand, for every man has his work cut out if we want to get out of this fuss with whole skins."

He spoke cheerily, but I afterwards learnt he was almost distracted when on the arrival of the rescue party, too late as he feared, we had been found bound to the altar stone.

I staggered to my feet, and, dizzy and faint from the effects of being in a cramped position during those terrible hours, I had great difficulty to prevent myself from falling, but a draught from a tin pannikin revived me wonderfully. My sporting rifle was hopelessly lost, so, picking up a revolver and a well-filled bandolier, I made my way across the courtyard to where the Maxim was trained ready to open fire.

The natives had gathered in a dense and disorderly mob around the chief's house and were making preparations to rush the gateway of the stockade. There were, I should think, nearly a thousand of them, against which a little band of Britishers, fifteen in all, had an almost superhuman task to perform, the result of which was to be either victory or a dreadful death.

"Steady, lads! Here they come!"

The two men at the Maxim, cool and collected, worked as calmly as if taking part in a sham fight.

"Commence!"

How shall I describe the terrible scene that followed?

Pop-pop-pop! Pop-pop-pop! The cartridge belt with its string of 250 rounds of .303 ammunition began to run swiftly through the breech-block, and from the water-jackets the steam rose in a thick cloud.

The centre of the dense mass of natives was literally crushed and beaten to the earth, but with redoubled shouts the flanks converged on the gate. At the critical moment there was a sudden pause in the firing—the Maxim had jammed!

Rapidly the men withdrew the belt, to find that a badly placed cartridge had projected sufficiently to prevent its passing through the breech; but even as they were thus engaged the foremost of the savages were almost within striking distance of the gate.

In obedience to a hoarse order the rest of the men temporarily forsook their stations at the loopholes, and, doubling up with fixed bayonets, poured in a rapid magazine fire upon the dense mass, while the deeper crack of the Webleys added to the deafening noise.

With a reckless disregard of their own safety; the natives, brandishing their terrible sharks'-toothed swords and spears, rushed dauntlessly towards the gate. Some, bearing the bodies of their slain comrades, strove to cast them upon the bayonets to break down the line of glittering steel; others, trusting to the protection afforded by their shields, found to their cost that fanatical bravery was useless before the weapons of the white man.

In the struggle we did not come of scatheless. One of the seamen, Barnes, lay on the ground, his leg transfixed with a jagged spear; nevertheless he continued firing, emptying his magazine with undiminished energy. Another, though who it was I was at the time unable to see, was doubled up in a heap by the side of the Maxim, while others received wounds of a less serious nature.

Notwithstanding the hot rifle and revolver fire, the savages kept up the attack with indomitable courage till, the jam having been cleared, the Maxim reopened fire, and under the withering blast the attackers melted and dispersed in utter disorder, leaving over a hundred of their number piled in ghastly heaps before the gate. Nor did they cease their headlong flight till well out of range.

The moment the fight was over, the doctor began his work of succouring the wounded. Barnes's case was by far the worst, as the fearful wound caused by the triple-headed spear had severed an artery, while Dr. Conolly had reason to suspect that the weapon was poisoned. Being without medical appliances, all that could be done for the sufferer was to apply a rough tourniquet, carefully wash the wound, and place a temporary bandage round the limb. The other man, who turned out to be Hinks, the "No. 1" of the Maxim, had been stunned by a large stone thrown at close range; but by a liberal application of cold water, of which there was fortunately a good supply, he was revived.

"We must get back to the ship as soon as possible," said my father. "The ammunition will run short if we stay here much longer."

"Let's hope they won't attack us on the way," replied the bos'n. "With two badly wounded men it would be hard for us."

"Yes, two men as stretcher-bearers to carry each of them, and two for the Maxim. That leaves but seven able to bear arms."

"Do you propose to burn the village? It would serve to impress the lesson more deeply."

"No; I think the poor fellows have suffered enough. Look upon the case from their point of view. Suppose, for instance, a party of niggers interfered with us at home—committed sacrilege, and otherwise trod on the corns of our feelings—wouldn't you cut up rough? Yet Conolly, by potting their sacred water-god, or whatever they call it, set the whole swarm of them buzzing round our heads. It's natural, after all. But there is one thing I'll burn, however."

"And that is——?"

"The idol."

Two stout levers were placed under the base of the grinning image, and with a hearty cheer the men bent to their work, and the ponderous mass of painted wood trembled, swayed for a few moments, then pitched headlong on the ground.

My father bent over it to more closely examine the painted and befeathered object. Suddenly he gave an exclamation of surprise.

"Herbert," he called to his brother, "come here and tell us what you think of this."

"Why," replied my uncle, "it's a figure-head."

"It is, or rather was. But it is more than that. See, the pedestal is carved with long staves, each surmounted by a cross."

"Well?"

"A cross-surmounted pole is the symbol of St. Philip the Apostle; consequently, unless I am much mistaken, the idol was at one time the figurehead of the 'San Philipo.' Of course, we cannot take it with us now; but, should an opportunity occur, I mean to have this relic on board the 'Fortuna.' Is everything ready, Mr. Wilkins?"

"Yes, sir."

"Very well; we'll try and make our way back to the ship."

A final examination showed that there were no signs of the natives in the vicinity of the village; so, taking the two wounded men on stretchers roughly improvised from bamboo poles and belts, we began our retreat.

It was a nerve-racking ordeal. From the pitiless glare of the sun the narrow path looked black and forbidding under the trees, and with the possibility that every thicket concealed a bloodthirsty enemy, every man was keenly on the alert. The snapping of a twig or the passage of a bird amongst the treetops caused the men to halt, with rifle at the ready, in anticipation of a fierce onslaught from an unseen foe; while, to add to our difficulties, Hinks began to show symptoms of lightheadedness, shouting and struggling so violently that he had to be strapped to the litter, while Barnes groaned loudly at each jolt of the stretcher.

But nothing of a hostile nature occurred, and at length, after a tedious two hours' march, we emerged from the wood and reached the beach; and it is doubtful whether Xenophon's Ten Thousand hailed the sight of the sea with greater delight than we did. For there lay the "Fortuna," riding easily to her anchor.

In obedience to a signal the two men who had been left on board manned the whaler and pulled for the beach, and ten minutes later the boat, heavily laden, was making its way back to the yacht.

Worn out with the effects of our terrible experience, we spent the rest of the day in idleness. For my part, after a good lunch, I turned in and slept till next morning, although once or twice I woke up in a bath of perspiration, the outcome of that horrible night.

Half an hour later we were over the scene of operations, and the divers immediately descended. It was a slow, tedious task, the clearing away of the weed and silt over the deck of the wreck, but before we could use a blasting charge it was necessary to thoroughly explore the hull, in order to make sure that the wreck was not too rotten to withstand the explosion.

Two hours elapsed, and the divers ascended, reporting good progress, but a lot of work lay before them, the tendrils of seaweed proving stubborn guardians of the hidden treasure; still, already they had made a passage to within a few feet of where the main hatch should be. After the midday meal down went the divers again for another two hours, and to me, sitting in the whaler, the monotony was most trying. Seeking for rich cargoes is all very well when one is taking an active part in the search, but when it comes to sitting in an open boat all day, literally with arms folded, and not knowing what is taking place beneath you, the enforced idleness soon palls even on the most sanguine spirits.

Next day came the same round of comparative idleness, save for the divers, who laboured incessantly, and the men at the pumps.

Another trying day came, and then, just before sunset, we were startled by hearing a terrific shouting on the beach. Bringing glasses to bear on the spot, we found that the natives had rejected their idol, which was indeed the figurehead of the "San Philipo," and had dragged it down to the sea shore, believing it to belong to the white men. However that may be, there it lay in the sand. The pater there and then determined that he would carry it home with him. As with the treasure of the sunken ship, he felt he had a certain proprietary right in the "San Philipo" and all belonging to her.

Chapter XVI

TOUCH AND GO

"I DON'T like the look of it," remarked my father, lightly tapping the barometer with his little finger. "A rapid rise, then up and down like a see-saw, followed by a still more rapid fall."

"Twenty-eight point four five—a drop of one point five, two inches in fifteen hours," observed Dr. Conolly. "It certainly looks as if something is in the air, though everything appears favourable at present."

"We'll be on the safe side and take every possible precaution," rejoined my father. "We are protected by the reef, so it will be as well to remain here, rather than get to sea and meet a cyclone in the open."

This conversation occurred about a fortnight after the arrival of the figurehead of the "San Philipo." The figurehead, or idol, we found too large conveniently to stow away on board, so it was cut through just below the shoulders, and, relieved of its accumulated coats of paint, the art of the Spanish wood-carver stood revealed once more to the light of day.

The actual head and bust of the great figurehead we took on board, lashing it securely in the main saloon, although even its present bulk, being four feet in height and three feet across the widest part, seriously interfered with the space we had at our disposal. As for the natives, they were now quiet enough. The heavy losses they had sustained had for the time being, at least, crushed their spirits, and we were able, with due precautions, to land whenever we wished.

Although on this particular morning everything seemed peaceful and quiet, the erratic behaviour of the mercury gave us ample warning that some great atmospheric disturbance was about to take place. Work on the wreck was in consequence suspended, the boats were hoisted in and secured all deck fittings lashed down, and an additional anchor with the longest possible scope was laid out.

About eight bells (4 p.m.) a heavy swell set in from seaward, although there was no wind to cause it, and all along the reef the dull round waves broke into great masses of foam with a noise like thunder, while the "Fortuna" rolled sluggishly in the undulations within the lagoon.

The sun, surrounded by a misty halo, sank behind a cluster of high-banked clouds, giving out strange copper-coloured rays, while from seaward came a constant string of birds, intent upon gaining the shelter of the land; and all the while a strange brooding silence appeared to have taken possession of the air, save for the roar of the breakers on the reef and the lesser noise of the water tumbling on the beach.

Hardly had the sun set than a heavy rain beat straight down, rattling on the decks (for we had taken in the awnings) and making a strange phosphorescent light on the water; but still there was no sign of wind.

"When the rain's before the wind,
Halliards, sheets, and braces bind."

"I wonder if that rhyme applies to this part of the globe?" remarked my uncle, as, clad in oilskins and sou'-westers, we stood' on deck, glad of the opportunity of being cooled by the downpour after weeks of tropic heat.

"We'll have it before long," said my father, looking towards the reef and trying to pierce the inky blackness. "And, in spite of the reef, we are on a lee shore.

"But not entirely open to the sea."

"No, but there'll be trouble if the anchors come home. By the by, did you stow away those blasting charges carefully?"

"I had them sent ashore and buried near the cave."

"That's good. I don't like the idea of having highly charged explosives on board in heavy electrical storms."

"Neither did I. Ha! What's that?"

Looking up, we saw a pale blue light flickering on our main-mast head, and for the moment I thought the vessel had taken fire.

"The air is full of electricity," said my father. "St. Elmo's Fires I think the sailors term the phenomenon. Reggie, run below out of the way. If you turn in before I see you again, turn in all standing, for you might be wanted on deck in a hurry."

I turned to obey, but just as I gained the companion the whole sky seemed one blaze of bluish light pierced by vivid flashes of lightning, which was immediately succeeded by a deafening peal of thunder that shook the yacht like a dried leaf in an October gale.

Even as I gained the cabin a furious blast struck the ship broadside on, and, staggering and pitching, she slewed round head to wind. The storm had broken.

Rolling, heaving, jumping short to her tautened cables, the "Fortuna" was fairly caught, and, down below, the sensation of being thrown about like a cork was almost worse than taking one's chances on deck. Reading was an utter impossibility, and all I could do was to wedge myself into my bunk, holding on when an extra heavy lurch threatened to hurl me across the cabin.

Just before midnight my father came below to swallow a hasty meal. The direction of the storm was, he told me, rapidly veering, for in these regions north of the Equator the gyration of these cyclones invariably takes place in one direction—from right to left, against the hands of a watch; while in the Southern Hemisphere the direction is reversed.

"We are on a weather shore at present," he added; "but before long we shall find ourselves on a lee shore, and the motion will be worse."

It was rather cold comfort, for already the pitching was more than I cared about.

At sunrise the wind was blowing dead on shore, and the mountainous breakers, sweeping over the reef, rolled with but slightly diminished force towards the land. The "Fortuna" was naturally head to wind, and riding in a totally opposite direction from that of the previous night, though, thanks to a massive swivel, she was free from the disadvantage of a "foul hawse."

To ease the strain on the cables the motor was started, and, alternately racing and biting as the propeller was lifted clear of the water or else submerged feet below the normal depth, the powerful little engine added its quota of noise to the howling of the elements.

For'ard everything was battened down, but the main companion hatch was left slightly open to admit fresh air to the cabin, and as sea after sea swept over our decks I could hear the ponderous blows of the masses of solid water as they flung themselves against the stout framework of the hatchway, on the lee side of which the watch on deck sheltered themselves as much as possible from the fury of the storm.

Slowly the hours passed; yet, although long after sunrise, the thick black clouds made the atmosphere so dark that it was impossible to see much farther than the length of the yacht, while flash after flash of lightning momentarily pierced the sombre gloom.

At the height of the storm the dreadful cry arose, "The anchors are coming home!" And this proved only too true, for our ground tackle was slowly dragging over the sandy bottom of the lagoon, and four hundred yards astern was the coral beach, on which the breakers would smash the "Fortuna" into matchwood in less than five minutes.

At the first alarm I rushed on deck, and, holding on like grim death to a belaying pin, I remained, washed by several successive seas, most of the crew doing likewise and grimly awaiting the end.

Suddenly there was a tremendous shock, as if the vessel had struck, and in the glare of a vivid flash we perceived that bearing down on us was a huge wave the like of which I had never seen before, and want never to see again. Fifty feet in height, the steep, unbroken mass rushed towards the "Fortuna," and, expecting her to be wrenched from her cables and buried beneath tons of green seas, we tightened our grip and gazed with feelings akin to panic on the approaching wave.

Above the roar of the oncoming water I heard my father shout, "Down below, all of you! It's our only chance!" and I was conscious of being dragged to the shelter of the companion, down which a scurrying stampede took place to gain a doubtful shelter.

The next instant the "Fortuna" seemed to literally stand upon end; we were all hurled, a struggling mass of humanity, against the after bulkhead, which to all intents and purposes became the floor. Then, after hours, as it seemed, of sickening suspense, during which we were in doubt as to whether the vessel still floated or was being borne down to the bottom of the lagoon, the "Fortuna" pitched forward till we were in danger of being thrown to the other end of the saloon, while on deck we could hear the ominous crash of broken wood and the sound of water pouring through the scuppers. Then, except for a slight roll, the yacht became as steady as if at anchor in a landlocked harbour.

With an exclamation of astonishment the bos'n dashed up the companion, and, without waiting to slide back the hatch, eeled himself through the narrow opening and gained the deck, the rest of us following closely.

A scene of confusion met our eyes. The mizzen-mast, broken off close to the deck, lay over our starboard quarter; part of the rail on the port bow was torn away, and the gig, wrenched from its strong lashings, was wedged against the fore side of the companion, with several of its planks stove in. But the cause of the bos'n's astonishment was the fact that right ahead of the "Fortuna," and less than two hundred yards away, was an enormous ledge of rock, some twenty to forty feet in height, stretching in front of us like a stone wall, its extremities lost in the semi-gloom, forming a natural breakwater.

Although the storm still raged furiously, and the showers of spray rose beyond the rock and fell like hissing rain right over us, the yacht lay under the lee of the newly formed barrier, fretting at her cables, which were now rubbing under her fore-foot.

"Stop the engine and have that wreckage cleared away," said my father. "We are safe enough for the present" and, with a sailor's instinct, the work of making things ship-shape was first taken in hand, before attempting to find out what act of Providence was responsible for our marvellous escape from being dashed to pieces on a lee shore.

The men set to work with a will. The broken mizzen-mast was cut clear and allowed to float at the end of a strong rope at a safe distance from our counter; the gig was secured, and things made ship-shape between decks, where the damage, though the confusion was indescribable, was confined to a few breakages of glass and china ware. Barely had the work of clearing up been completed than the storm ceased, almost as suddenly as it had begun, and the sun shone forth in a cloudless sky. We could now form some idea of what had occurred to turn the heaving waters of the lagoon into a sheltered harbour. Where but a few hours before had been a low coral reef, a long, irregular ledge of rock had been thrown up from the bed of the sea, and although its upper surface was composed of weed-covered stone and fragments of corals, its landward face was as fresh and clear as if cut by a gigantic chisel, and the highest part was where the entrance to the lagoon had been.

But the greatest surprise of all was that, wedged in an almost upright position, the weed-covered wreck of the "San Philipo" lay exposed to the light of day, after resting for nearly two centuries at the bottom of the sea. In spite of the clinging masses of weed the line of her double row of ports could be distinctly traced, while, owing to her slight list, we could see her sloping decks, built like a succession of broad steps rising from her waist. Her lofty stern, with its projecting galleries, was practically intact, and the only part that destroyed the graceful symmetry of her hull was for'ard, where the bows, torn by a long-standing injury, terminated in a tangle of broken planks and jagged timbers.

The crew looked with awestruck astonishment at this relic of the deep. It was as if they had been transported back to the beginning of the eighteenth century to see this antiquated object of naval architecture suddenly placed before their eyes; but my father looked upon the spectacle from a practical point of view. "It's saved us an awkward task," he remarked.

"What has?" I inquired.

"Reggie, my boy, you have seen what few of the inhabitants of the globe have seen before—the birth of an island. There has been a violent volcanic disturbance, and a portion of the submarine bed has been forced upwards, forming the mass of rock that you can see before you. Such instances are rare, but by no means unknown. That huge wave that all but overwhelmed the 'Fortuna' was caused by the sudden distortion of the earth's crust, which, generally speaking, is weakest along the western shore of the Pacific Ocean, though 'tis evident that the island is situated immediately above a centre of volcanic activity. It has been extremely fortunate for us, although, had the upheaval occurred but a few yards this way, it would have meant the death of us all."

"Do you think we shall have another shock?

"More than likely, though hardly so powerful. These seismic disturbances often occur in series, and it may be that the island will disappear as quickly as it came. However, we must take our chance, explore the wreck, and remove the treasure if it is to be found. Well, Mr. Wilkins?"

"Would you mind stepping for'ard, sir?"

The bos'n led the way to the fo'c'sle, and, looking over the bow, he showed us the cable, to which the yacht was riding easily.

"Well, what's wrong?" asked my father.

"Can you see below the swivel, sir?"

A further examination showed that one of the cables, composed of 3/4-in. galvanized chain, had parted just below the swivel, while the yacht now only rode to the second anchor.

"We'll send a diver after it directly the swell has gone down," said the bos'n. "And look astern, sir; it's been touch and go."

Within a cable's length a ridge of jagged, teeth-like rocks showed in the trough of each gentle undulation. A mass of rock had been recently fired up from the bed of the lagoon, for previously its floor was remarkably free from obstructions, so that, had the remaining cable parted, the "Fortuna" would have been dashed to pieces on this new danger, and her crew, even had they escaped from this peril, would have teen ground by the remorseless breakers against the shore of the island.

Some idea of the violence of the cyclone could be gathered from the fact that the huge tidal wave had swept the beach and broken against the grove of coco-nut palms, for the trunks of the trees, some of which had been uprooted, were covered with trailing masses of seaweed and the remains of the islanders' canoes.

As I looked on the scene of desolation, the strewn beach and the rocky pinnacles astern of us, and thence on the protecting masses of our newly formed island, I realized more fully to what extent we owed our safety to Providence, arid, like the bos'n, I could express the situation in no other words than that "it's been touch and go with all of us."

Chapter XVII

WE FIND THE TREASURE

THERE was not much time for reflections; work, and pressing work too, had to be done. Under the bos'n's orders a party of men set about repairing the damaged gig and the broken rail, while on examination it was found that the broken mizzen-mast was practically unstrained beyond the actual fracture, so that, by cutting through and restepping the longest portion, a serviceable though somewhat stumpy mast would do duty until we could obtain a new spar at the nearest port. Three men under the orders of the quartermaster went off in the whaler to take soundings in the vicinity of the yacht's berth in order to become acquainted with the position of any fresh shoals or reefs; while the divers prepared to descend to try and recover the lost anchor and cable.

"I've just seen poor old Barnes," said Dr. Conolly, as he came on deck and joined us. "He's had a nasty time during the storm, and what I was afraid of has come about. He shows symptoms of blood-poisoning, and I must operate at once."

"Poor fellow! Poor fellow!" ejaculated my father. "I suppose he'll pull through?"

"He has a fighting chance, but you can rely upon me to do my very best. We must perform the operation on deck; so will you give orders for the awning to be rigged, and a screen placed athwart ship. We have plenty of fresh water, I think?"

"Yes, plenty. I'll have the awning rigged at once."

This news startled me, for when last I saw the wounded man he seemed on the fair road to recovery. But no time was to be lost. The awning was rigged, a rough table placed on the fo'c'sle, and a bucket of water, an array of surgical instruments (which the doctor had bought during our stay at Malta), and boxes of surgical dressing and linen completed the hasty preparations.

The divers were told to divest themselves of their diving-suits, and, after selecting three men to assist the doctor, my father ordered the rest away in the whaler, giving them instructions to sound carefully between the ledge of rocks and the shore, though this was merely an excuse to clear the ship during the actual operation.

Presently Barnes was brought on deck on a rough stretcher, the task of getting him through the fore-hatch proving one of great difficulty to the bearers and painful to the patient. They laid him on the table, and a nauseating smell that reminded me forcibly of old Dr. Trenoweth's surgery at Fowey seemed to fill the air.

"Clear out of this, Reggie!" said my Uncle Herbert peremptorily. "Go below and read a book, or do something. This is no place for you."

I went, but my thoughts were full of the poor sufferer lying on deck. Even the saloon reeked of the sickening odour, while through the open skylight I could hear every sound: the short, quick orders of the doctor, the splashing of the water, the convulsive movements of the insensible patient, the clatter of the instruments and even the sharp, rasping noise of the saw, and finally the distressing groans of the man as he recovered consciousness.

Then I heard the signal for the whaler, and presently the sound of the oars splashing alongside.

"Come along, my boy," exclaimed my father; "we are going off to the wreck." Gladly I left the cabin and got into the boat. Barnes still remained on deck, a bed being prepared for him under a square of canvas formed into a small tent. Dr. Conolly remained with his patient, but my father and uncle went in the whaler.

"There's a place where we can land, just on the other side of the wreck," said the bos'n; "but it's an awkward job."

This indeed it seemed, for the side of the newly made island was as steep and as smooth as polished rock, save for a few crevices and longitudinal cracks, so far apart as to be useless for climbing. A few strokes, however, brought us to the spot indicated by the bos'n, where the shattered bows of the "San Philipo" almost overhung the cliff. Here a flight of natural steps led up to within fifteen feet of the summit, but the whole of that fifteen feet was as smooth as a sheet of glass.

"Another fifty feet and the old hooker would have tumbled over the edge," observed the bos'n. "The whole place is one mass of ups and downs. Do you know, sir, that between the 'Fortuna' and the little reef astern of her—the new one, I mean—we found the bottom at a hundred fathoms, and between the reef and the shore, where there used to be from four to six fathoms, we found as much as sixty?"

"It's been a most tremendous upheaval," replied my father; "and I'm not surprised at anything after this. However, the question is: How are we to land?

"That's what I was thinking of, sir," replied Wilkins, knitting his brow. "How would bending the whaler's anchor on to a line and heaving it up do?"

"I am afraid that throwing up a twenty-four-pound anchor to a height of over twenty feet would be beyond the strength of most of us," observed my uncle, with a smile.

"Then heave the line over the wreck."

"The lead-line would not be strong enough to bear a man," objected my father. "The only thing to be done is to get a spar—the yard of our square-sail, for instance."

"A couple of young trees would do better, I'm thinking," said the bos'n. "We've plenty of lashing in the boat, and a ladder could be knocked up in a jiffey."

"The very thing, Mr. Wilkins. Make for the shore as fast as you can."

The whaler's bow grounded on the beach, and, making our way with difficulty through the debris that lined the seaward side of the grove, we selected a couple of young palm-trees. These were felled and cut to lengths of twenty feet, and the rungs firmly fastened, making a serviceable ladder. This we towed behind the boat, and on landing on the rock we scaled the perpendicular height with comparative ease.

The ladder was then hauled up and placed against the towering, weed-covered sides of the "San Philipo," and, led by my father, we all ascended and gained the deck of the wreck.

"Be careful, sir," cautioned the bos'n; "the deck may be rotten in places."

"All right, Mr. Wilkins," replied my father. "I see the divers have been hard at work, for the waist has practically been cleared."

But before attempting to go below, my father made his way aft, and, clambering cautiously over the successive breaks of the tiers of decks, reached the towering poop. Here the stump of the mizzen-mast still projected a couple of feet above the deck, while a litter of rotten rope trailed across the poop from the mizzen chains, and a rusty mass of iron alone remained to denote what had at one time been the three poop lanterns.

It was not, however, to this scene of desolation that my father's attention was directed. From the commanding position we had, for the first time, a complete view of the results of the upheaval, and to our consternation we found that the lagoon was converted into a land-locked sheet of water, huge rocks forming a massive semi-circular barrier from shore to shore. The "Fortuna" was a prisoner, and, to all intents and purposes, seemed doomed to lie within the lagoon till she rotted and sank at her moorings.

The original entrance had, as I have already mentioned, been closed up by lofty masses of rock, while throughout the whole length of the newly formed reef there was not, as far as we could see, any part less than twenty feet above the level of high water.

For several minutes my father stood looking at the scene with absolute dejection written on his face. It seemed as if all his hopes were shattered at one blow.

"Cheer up, old fellow," said his brother sympathetically, though he, too, was keenly alive to the extent of our misfortune. "It might be worse; we've got the yacht intact, the treasure under our feet, and, what is more, our lives have been miraculously preserved."

"Our lives, 'tis true. But what is the use of the treasure when the yacht is hopelessly imprisoned?"

"There's a saying, 'Don't holler till you're out of the wood'; it could have very well been added: 'Don't cry till you've tried to find a way out'; so don't worry till we've made a careful exploration of the reef. I suppose people at home have read a report in the daily papers before now, a telegram from Professor Milne to the effect that a great seismic disturbance has been recorded, the probable area affected being approximately eleven thousand miles away."

"Oh, yes," replied my father, with a slight suspicion of sarcasm. "Imagine the interest it causes to the majority of the British Public; but, so long as his pocket isn't touched, the average man doesn't care, even if half the surface of the globe is turned upside down; but let a cat or a dog scratch up his front garden——"

"Oh, for pity's sake stop moralizing. Let's make a start and explore the ship. See, the men have already nearly cleared away the mud from the main hatch."

Before long my father had shaken off his depression and was hard at work clearing the weed and sand. The hatches were forced open with crowbars, and we had our first view of the main deck. Considering the time the vessel had lain at the bottom of the sea, the amount of dirt and sand that had worked its way between decks was remarkably small; but on descending the ladder it seemed as if we were in a broad, low-roofed cave.

Through the gun-ports, now festooned with seaweed, the sunlight filtered, causing a thick, nauseating mist to rise from the sodden timbers; while on the starboard side was a tangled collection of timber and iron, the remains of the ship's ordnance, all the iron guns having been reduced to a softness resembling plumbago; but eight pieces of brass ordnance still retained their original appearance, save for the discoloration caused by the action of the salt water.

"Let's see what there is in the cabins aft," said Uncle Herbert, making for a half-open door; "I suppose no one brought a lantern?—it's pitch dark."

Even as he spoke the door creaked and moved slowly inwards, while a strange rustling noise was heard in the alley-way. Jumping backwards, my uncle raised an axe that he was carrying, and assumed a defensive attitude, while the rest of us, in breathless expectancy, awaited developments.

Again the shuffling noise was repeated, and out of the darkness projected a long, greenish hued, repulsive-looking object, terminating in a pair of formidable nippers, and in another moment a gigantic crab, fully five feet across its shell, shambled out of the gloom, turned partly over on its side to pass the doorway, and made straight for us.

"Call yourself a Cornishman, and afraid of a crab!" exclaimed my father as my uncle turned and ran for safety.

But it was not a cause for jest. One of the men stabbed at the creature with a crowbar, but, seizing the iron between its formidable claws, the monster wrenched it from the man's grasp, nearly throwing him to the deck. Another struck a heavy blow with an axe, but the steel seemed to have no effect upon the tough armour of the brute's shell, and it was clear that a man would stand little chance if caught by those powerful nippers.

"Hack off his legs!" shouted the bos'n, and, snatching an axe from one of the seamen, he put all his strength into a powerful cut at the creature's leg. The steel bit deeply into the member, but, before the bos'n could withdraw the axe, the crab spun round, swept the bos'n off his feet, and made for its prostrate antagonist, who, wedged against the ship's side, had no chance of escape. But before the hideous brute could accomplish its object, Lord, the quartermaster, made a bound, and alighted on its shell, and with his axe dealt two smashing blows at the creature's eyes. This interference caused the crab to swerve from its purpose, and, raising itself, threw the quartermaster to keep company with the bos'n.

Taking advantage of the raised position of the brute, my father fired three shots in quick succession from his revolver straight into its head, and, having had more than it cared about, the crab retreated for its den, but, before it reached the doorway, it stopped, gave a few convulsive struggles, and fell dead, a thin stream of pale-coloured blood trickling over the slimy decks into the debris on the lee side.

"Hot work while it lasted," remarked my father, ejecting the three empty cylinders and reloading his revolver. "Move the thing out of the way, and let's explore the cabins. I hope there are no more of that sort, though."

One of the men had returned with a lantern from the whaler, and by its aid we began our tour of the cabins and state-rooms. There were multitudes of crabs, large and small, though none approaching in size the one we had killed; several small cuttlefish squirmed in the mud that was ankle-deep on the floors; while overhead the mouldering beams were alive with immense worms, gliding in and out of the innumerable tunnels they had eaten in the timbers.

Most of the cabin doors were locked, but so rotten was the woodwork that a kick was sufficient to demolish them. The first five or six were practically empty, though one contained a number of brass-hilted swords, all in a more or less rust-eaten condition. At length we came to one over which were the letters "...apitan."

"This ought to contain something worth having, being the captain's," remarked my uncle, bursting open the door. Compared with the rest of the cabins this apartment was large and well-lighted, the stern window being fairly free from the trailing weeds.

Rotting curtains still hung from the walls; furniture that for nearly two centuries had floated against the once-gilded ceiling had fallen in utter confusion on the mud-covered floor, while there was the usual scurrying of swarms of shell-fish, as they sought shelter in the darker recesses of the room. In the centre stood two massive chests, bound with iron, and to these my father hastened, ignoring the crabs that impeded his footsteps.

"Hurry up with the crowbar!" he exclaimed excitedly, and, inserting the iron bar underneath the lid, he put his whole strength into the task of prizing open one of the chests.

With all his powerful efforts the lid defied him, and, calling the bos'n to his aid, both of them bent to the stout lever. The wood creaked and groaned, yet neither did the chest move nor did the lid fly open.

"There's weight in it!" exclaimed the bos'n, wiping his heated brow. "If we are not careful the whole box of tricks will fall through into the hold."

"Yes, we must look out for that," replied my father; "already the floor seems to be giving."

"More than the lid does, I'm thinking," assented the bos'n. "We must try what a sledge-hammer and wedges will do." This meant sending back to the "Fortuna"; so, while the whaler was away, we continued our exploration of the cabin. There were three silver images, blackened by sea-water, several gold and silver-mounted sword-hilts, a drawer full of gold coins, bearing dates between 1590 and 1701, tankards and plates of precious metal, and several securely sealed bottles, containing, as we afterwards found, wine.

"Ah! now we can tackle the chests," exclaimed Uncle Herbert, as the men returned with a sledge-hammer and a regular armoury of cold chisels. "This one first."

A few heavy blows and the lid flew open; then, by the aid of the crowbar, the work was completed, and the lid went back with a loud creaking sound. The chest was filled to the brim with small bars of solid gold.

"Hurrah, my lads!" shouted my father in his excitement. "This alone will repay us. You can take it from me that once we get this safely home, every man of the crew will be able to live in comfort till the end of his days."

A rousing cheer greeted this announcement; then, closing the lid, my father directed the men to burst open the other chest.

This we found to contain mostly silk-stuffs, all, of course, utterly spoiled by age and sea-water; but at the bottom was a complete set of Church plate, made of gold and blazing with precious stones.

"Some cathedral in Spain is the poorer by this," remarked Uncle Herbert, holding up a massive chalice to the glassless stern window and allowing the light to play on the dazzling stones. "What do you propose to do, Howard? I don't think we can rest at ease till the whole of this stuff is safely aboard the 'Fortuna.'"

"Neither can we. We'll explore the hold now, and directly afterwards we'll begin to tranship the contents of the chests."

"We must lose no time, then, for it will take the rest of the day."

A hasty examination of the hold showed us that the silver cargo of the "San Philipo" was no myth; the ballast was composed of solid silver "pigs."

"We'll return to the 'Fortuna' now," decided my father. "You, Herbert, had better superintend the shifting of the contents of the chests. Tomorrow, if all's well, we'll tackle the silver, and, if the gig's repaired, four men and the bos'n can explore the reef."

Chapter XVIII

COMMITTED TO THE DEEP

"I'M afraid it's a case with poor Barnes," said Dr. Conolly, in a low tone, as the whaler came alongside the yacht and my father climbed over the side. "He's taken a turn for the worse, and I don't think he'll last till tomorrow.

"Poor fellow! Is there no hope?"

The doctor shook his head. "I was doubtful from the first. The spear was a poisoned one; though the poison was undoubtedly stale, and therefore slow in action, it was none the less sure."

"Can he be seen?"

"Yes, he's quite conscious."

I followed my father to the shelter-tent, under which the wounded seaman lay.

"Well, Barnes, how goes it—better?" he asked, with a forced cheerfulness.

"No, sir, though 'tain't no good making a fuss about it. My number's up."

"Nonsense, man! you'll soon be all right again, I hope."

"All right aloft, sir, please God. I'm real glad you've come to see me, Cap'n, for there'll be one or two little things I want squared up."

"I'll do anything I can."

"Well, sir, there's my medal for South Africa, with three clasps: would you mind accepting it as a kind o' keepsake from me? An' there's the good-conduct medal, too. That ain't of much account compared with t'other, but p'r'aps Mister Reginald would 'ave it."

"Thank you, Barnes; but have you no friends to give them to?"

"Never a relation in the world, sir. There's my pension papers in my ditty-box; it's a matter of three quarters due to me. Will you see that my chum, Joe Dirham, draws it? I've signed a paper about it."

"All right; I'll see to that."

"An' my identity-paper. It'll fetch a shilling at the 'Register's' at the first home-port we touch. Joe might just as well 'ave that; 'tain't no good throwin' good money away, and, besides, it will make all square and above-board up at the Admiralty."

"Do you feel much pain?"

"Precious little, Cap'n. As I said afore, it's no good makin' a fuss over it; a seaman with one leg ain't of no use to you, but"—here his voice trembled a little—"promise me, sir, that you'll bury me at sea, an' not on the island; it'll be a snug moorin' for me at the bottom of the lagoon. Now, Cap'n, read somethin' out of the Book, an' say a prayer for me—I, never wasn't much in that line myself."

Somehow I felt unable to remain longer, so, shaking the seaman's thin hand, I went aft, leaving my father with him.

The news of the state of poor Barnes cast a gloom over the ship, and any feeling of enthusiasm over the discovery of the treasure was smothered by the melancholy reflection that one of our comrades was on his deathbed.

Next morning I was awakened by the sound of voices on deck. The sun had risen in a thick haze, and, though not a zephyr disturbed the surface of the lagoon, the air was cool and pleasant. Wondering what the sounds meant, and whether poor Barnes had gone, I slipped on my clothes and went on deck.

Clustered round the tent were most of the crew, listening to the voice within, or whispering to each other in subdued tones. I went forward, and found my father, Dr. Conolly, and the bos'n standing by the side of the temporary bunk on which poor Barnes lay. The dying seaman was fighting his battles o'er again, shouting and talking in clear yet hurried tones. Now he was in the sweltering heat of a West African backwater, advancing with his shipmates to storm the stockade of a rebel chieftain; next he was serving a 4.7 gun with the Naval Brigade, his feeble hands clutching in grim pretence at the handspikes as the huge weapon on its unwieldy carriage was trained on the advancing Boers. Other episodes followed in quick succession, till the scene in the stockade where he received his fatal wound' seemed to exhaust his last flickering strength.

"Can't you see it's getting quite dark?" he exclaimed feebly. "What's wrong with the bos'n's mate? Why, hain't he piped the lamp-trimmers? ...Ah! that's better; the anchor-lamp's burnin' now, so we're brought up at last.... Turn it up a little, lads... That's it... Burning brightly now..."

The words died away in a long-drawn sigh. The doctor bent over the now motionless form' and placed a finger lightly on one eye. Then he shook his head. "Cover him over, poor fellow; he's made his last voyage and reached the port aloft."

* * * * *

Two hours later, the whaler pushed off from the side of the "Fortuna," with almost ever, man on board, and a still, shrouded form, covered with a Union Jack, lying on a board athwartships, the grand and solemn words of the Burial Service for use at sea mingling with the soft splash of the oars as the men, keeping slow time, pulled the boat towards the deepest part of the lagoon.

"... Suffer us not, at our last hour, for any pains of death, to fall from Thee."

"Way enough; toss oars," ordered the bos'n in a low tone.

The men raised their oars to a vertical position, as a last tribute to their shipmate, and the boat gradually began to lose way.

"... We therefore commit his body to the deep, to be turned into corruption, looking for the resurrection of the body, when the sea shall give up its dead...."

The bos'n gave the signal, and the board was tilted up, and with a slight splash, the shrouded form slid into the water, leaving the Union Jack fluttering in the boat. Instinctively I looked over the side, and followed the course of the weighted canvas that enclosed the mortal remains of poor Barnes, till the grey shroud turned a greenish tinge, and at length was lost in the depth of the lagoon. With heavy hearts we rowed back to the yacht.

* * * * *

Needless to say there was no work done on the wreck for the rest of that day, but, to banish the feeling of depression, all hands were kept busily employed, some on the repairs to the gig, others making and repairing canvas gear, while the two divers made a successful descent and recovered the lost anchor and cable. On coming up they reported that the anchor was actually balanced on the edge of a deep chasm, it being only by the merest chance that the ground tackle had not been irrecoverably lost. So delicate, in fact, was the position of the anchor, that the divers hesitated to approach it for fear that it might make a sudden descent and carry them with it over the abyss.

Just before sunset a strong party went ashore to refill the barricoes. The doctor and I went with them, but no amount of persuasion could induce Yadillah to set foot upon the island again, and during our stay he kept firmly to his resolution. We noticed a curious fact in connection with the journey ashore. The water was tinged in colour, and had a strong, sulphurous smell, so that we argued there must have been a volcanic outlet somewhere in the neighbourhood, or, failing that, there was a tremendous natural agency still bottled up beneath the island, that before long must seek to escape by another violent upheaval.

* * * * *

Soon after daybreak on the following day the working-parties set out on their varied tasks, for, on account of the heat between the sea-soddened timbers of the wreck, it was decided to suspend work during the hottest part of the day.

The whaler's crew, under the orders of my uncle, devoted themselves to the unloading and transporting of the iron pigs from the hold of the "Fortuna," intending to replace them with bars of solid silver from the "San Philipo"; while a party of men, under my father and the bos'n, went away in the now serviceable gig to survey the reef.

I chose to go with the gig, which was certainly a more pleasant amusement than working inside a steaming wreck, for even at that early hour a thick vapour enveloped the "San Philipo."

For some distance the two boats kept company, the lighter boat towing a pair of sheers which were to be set up on the cliff to enable the pigs to be handled the more easily, while the whaler, in addition to being heavily laden with ballast from the yacht, carried a second pair of sheers to set up over the main hatchway of the wreck.

Opposite the landing-place on the reef we cast off our share of the gear and rowed slowly by the ledge of rocks, my father keeping a sharp eye on the formation of the reef to see if any of the gaping crevices actually led to the open sea beyond.

For nearly a mile and a half the rock rose sheer from the water's edge, and although the boat was backed into several winding gaps in the reef, in every case the attempt to find a channel proved fruitless. As we approached the spot where the reef joined the island, the rocks became lower, but the depth of water was so little, and the shoal extended so far from the reef, that it would have been impossible to bring the yacht up to the reef, even if a channel existed.

"Try the other end of the lagoon, sir," advised the bos'n. "We've let that part alone up to the present."

"There's no harm in trying, Mr. Wilkins," replied my father, "though, if I remember rightly, the original coral reef was very irregular at that part, and stretched seawards for a considerable distance."

When, after an hour's steady pulling, we arrived at the other end of the reef, we found that the rock was very similar to the rest, being pierced by many deep channels that, as usual, terminated in what the bos'n termed "blind alleys."

Three of these were explored without success, but the fourth, some twenty feet in width in its narrowest part, ran in a straight direction for nearly a hundred yards, the walls on either side gradually diminishing in height from twenty-five to less than ten feet. Its end terminated in a mass of broken stone, deposited as if by human agency, in a diagonal direction, affording great facilities for climbing.

"It strikes me, sir," remarked Mr. Wilkins, "that the sea is only a few feet beyond the rock. Listen! you can hear the waves bleating against the seaward side."

It certainly struck the bos'n, but in a totally different manner from that which he implied, for, without warning, a terrific blast of air, followed by a column of water, was forced through an orifice in the rock, Mr. Wilkins, who was standing upon one of the thwarts in order to make a more complete survey, being in the direct line of fire, received the full force of the discharge, and was knocked completely over the side of the boat, while the rest of us were drenched to the skin.

The unfortunate bos'n was quickly hauled on board, little the worse for his ducking, and the gig was backed off beyond the danger zone.

"Experience does it!" gasped the bos'n, spitting out a mouthful of water; "which is, I am told, the Latin for 'Experience makes fools wise.' Am I not right, Mr. Reginald?"

"Well, what has experience taught you?" asked my father, laughing.

"Only what I thought was the case before," replied the bos'n. "And that is, that there's a communication through this rock between the lagoon and the open sea."

"I don't see how that can help us," remarked my father.

"May be, may be not, sir," observed Mr. Wilkins oracularly. "But if you don't mind, sir, will you land here for a few minutes. We can manage it quite easily by the broken rocks at the side of the blowing-hole."

We gained the summit of the reef without much difficulty. Here, as the bos'n had expressed his opinion, a ledge, barely six feet in width, separated us from the open sea, while on either hand, at a distance of less than a hundred yards, a long reef ran at right angles to the main ledge, terminating in jagged points of disrupted coral nearly half a mile from where we stood.

By the deep-blue colour of the water it was evident that there was plenty of depth between these two natural groynes, which formed ample protection from the heavy rollers that at every other point along the reef broke with a ceaseless roar.

"You've got your revolver with you, I see, sir," said the bos'n. "I'm going to dive off and see what the rock looks like on the seaward side. There may be sharks about and there may not; but keep a bright look-out, and fire at one if it comes for me. Money," he added to the bowman of the gig, "unreeve the painter and sling it ashore, will you."

"There, sir," he continued, "I'll take a turn round the rock, and drop the free end of the rope in the water so that I can pull myself up; but keep a bright look-out, if you please."

Hastily divesting himself of his sodden garments, and placing them to dry on the hot stones, the bos'n took a magnificent "header," and cleft the water with hardly a splash. Quite two fathoms down he went before he turned and swam towards the rocky wall, keeping below the water at the same depth. Half a minute later he reappeared, and, shaking the water from his hair, he grasped the rope and came up hand over hand.

"That's all right, sir. Deep water both sides, and the rock full of holes."

"What do you mean?" asked my father, unable to grasp the meaning of the bos'n's words.

"Why, sir, the 'Fortuna' can float easily on either side of this little neck of rock."

"On one side, I'll grant."

"Aye, on both sides, once we make a way through."

"Oh, how do you propose to do it'? Remove each piece of rock bit by bit, when the weight of the smallest is two tons at the very least—eh?"

"No, sir," replied the bos'n.

"Then how are you going to set about it?"

"Blast it," said Mr. Wilkins emphatically.

Chapter XIX

THE CAVE

THE bos'n's proposal was hailed with enthusiasm, for, curiously enough, neither my father nor my uncle had given any thought to the blasting powder the use of which is an everyday occurrence in the mining districts of Cornwall.

"How much of the stuff have we?" asked my father.

"Mr. Herbert had over fifty pounds of it carried ashore before the gale," replied the bos'n. "It's all in air-tight cases, so it won't be damaged by being buried."

"It's a wonder the whole lot hadn't exploded during the storm! There's enough rock brought down from the cliff to show that the shock was exceptionally severe, to say nothing of the chance of it being struck by lightning."

"But it hasn't, sir, so that is something to be thankful for. However, it would be well to finish unloading the ballast from the yacht, but not to take the silver aboard till we have blown up the rock and made a clear passage through."

"For what reason, Mr. Wilkins?"

"Simply because we don't know what depth the new cutting will be. It might be twelve feet, it might be only six; so the lighter we can make the vessel the less draught she'll draw, and the greater chance she'll have of slipping through."

"But there will be greater difficulty in loading up outside the reef."

"Granted, sir; but we must take the risk, unless, of course, the blasting-powder cuts a deep and unobstructed channel."

So, directly we returned to the "Fortuna," message was sent to the wreck to defer the removal of the pigs of silver for the present.

On my uncle's return he reported that the twenty sows were correct in number, but only ten chests full of pieces-of-eight were to be found, so it was assumed that the remaining five chests had been broken open and their contents shared out by Humphrey Trevena immediately after the capture of the "San Philipo" by the "Anne."

Nearly five tons of ballast had been removed from the "Fortuna," more than sufficient to compensate for the additional weight of the specie; but, in view of the probable difficulty of taking the yacht between the reefs to the open sea, it was decided to proceed with the unloading of the iron ballast, till the "Fortuna's" draught would be reduced to the least margin of safety.

"We've done very well this forenoon," remarked my father, "so we can reasonably take a spell off till the sun is low down."

"As you like, but, personally speaking, I have a perfect craving for hard work," replied Uncle Herbert, "so I'll beat up volunteers and recover the blasting powder."

"You won't bring it aboard?"

"No, I will take it off to the reef, close to the channel you mentioned."

"I'll go, too," I exclaimed, "for I want very much to have a look at the great cave that we can see from here."

"I don't think so," objected my uncle. "A boatload of explosives, powerful enough to blow, us to infinitesimal particles, is hardly a safe cargo, so you will be safer on board the 'Fortuna.'"

"I know, but you can take the stuff off to the reef and come back for me. It's only a ten minutes' pull, you know. Don't be hard on a fellow, uncle. It's the first time I've had a chance to go ashore in that part of the bay, and I want to explore the cave."

"Very well, then," replied my uncle ungraciously. "But mind, no monkey-tricks, and don't run into mischief."

I ran below to the bos'n's locker, where I abstracted a ball of seaming-twine and a couple of candles, and, putting these articles into my coat pocket in company with a box of matches, I went on deck and clambered into the gig.

The spot where the explosives had been buried was in a grove, a short distance from a little bay, which was enclosed on either hand by tall cliffs, and inaccessible from the rest of the lagoon except by means of a boat, unless a path was cut inland through the dense scrub, which apparently had never yet been penetrated by human beings.

The taller of the two cliffs was almost divided from base to summit by the curiously shaped cave which Old Humphrey had laid particular stress upon in his log, and directly the boat touched the sandy beach I bounded off towards it on my trip of exploration, a final warning from my uncle falling lightly upon my ears.

A heap of loose boulders, which had fallen during the shock, encumbered the mouth of the cave; but these I easily surmounted, and advanced cautiously over the smooth floor, my eyes dim by the sudden change from the brilliant sunshine to the subdued light of the cavern.

The walls were composed of blocks of basalt, the general regularity of the vertical shafts broken here and there by gaping horizontal and diagonal fissures, while at intervals a thin stream of water fell from the roof with a cool and pleasing sound.

As I proceeded the roof gradually became lower, till, just as the daylight failed, its height was less than twenty feet. Taking the ball of twine out of my pocket, I made fast one end to a projecting ledge. The candles, I found, had united into a soft bent stick of wax by reason of the heat of the sun, but, straightening them out and cooling them in a pool of water, I had a double-wicked torch in place of the two candles.

As I went on, making a careful survey of the ground for fear of pitfalls, I noticed that on either hand numerous side passages branched out, some large, some small; but, keeping as straight a direction as I could, I advanced slowly, paying out the twine as I went.

At length the smooth floor gave place to a ridge of rock, about four feet in height, leaving an opening of barely three feet between it and the roof. Here I stopped, debating with myself whether it would be wiser to retrace my way, but a feeling of uncontrollable curiosity urged me to continue my investigations.

Having unrolled a length of twine, I threw the ball over the barrier. Having one hand free, I began to clamber over the ridge, holding the lighted candle carefully in my left hand. Beyond I could see that the floor was even, though higher than on the side which I had left, so I unhesitatingly slipped down the opposite slope of the rock and gained the interior of the inner cave.

The light flickered on innumerable stalactites, which glittered like pinnacles and pendants of dazzling gems, while, for the first time, I became aware of the dismal silence and tomb-like solitude of the cave. I tried to whistle, but no sound came from my parched lips; then I called in a low tone, and to my surprise the echoes surpassed my voice in the volume of sound and then gradually died away, till it seemed as if, from the remote recesses of the cavern, came a mocking laugh.

I repeated the call, and again yet louder, when suddenly there was a rush and a roar, and I found myself lying on my back in utter darkness.

For some considerable time I lay helpless, the utter blackness and the terrifying solitude almost depriving me of my senses. Something heavy was gripping my left foot, and I found that I was held by a mass of fallen stone. The candle had been thrown from my hand, and was extinguished by the fall; but with feverish haste I drew the box of matches from my pocket and struck a light. Close at hand was the candle, and by its renewed light I saw, to my horror, that a fall had occurred from the roof, and my retreat was cut off by a tightly wedged mass of stone.

By a supreme effort I wrenched my foot free and staggered upright, stifling a desire to shout for fear that a further fall might occur. Hastily I tried to find a communication through the barrier, but there was no hope in that direction. Even the twine was held as firmly, as if tied to a post, and, on attempting to pull it, the thread broke off close to the rock.

I broke into a cold sweat, but after a few minutes I recovered my senses to a certain extent, arguing with myself that I should be missed before long, and that plenty of willing hands could remove that mass of rubble which held me prisoner.

The light, however, gave me grave misgivings, for the double-wicked candle was burning away rapidly, so, by the aid of my knife, I split the wax cylinder lengthways, thus giving me two candles, as I had originally. One I blew out and put in my pocket, with the feeling of satisfaction of having a light for six hours at the least.

Slowly the time passed. Surely, I thought, my uncle must have taken the explosives to the reef long before now; why had he not come to look for me? Fearful thoughts flashed through my bewildered brain. Supposing the blasting powder had exploded, blowing my uncle and the boat's crew to atoms. My father would naturally conclude that I had shared their fate, and I would be left to perish miserably in the awful darkness of this lonely cavern. Probably it was the detonation of the explosion and not the vibration of the sound of my voice that had dislodged the roof of the cave.

At length, after hours, as it seemed, of weary waiting, I heard a dull rumble in the direction of the mouth of the cavern, and gradually the sound came nearer and nearer.

"Can't go no 'igher, sir," came a faint voice. "The string stops 'ere, an' the whole place is broken up."

"Reggie! Reggie! Are you there?"

"I'm here, uncle. Don't shout, or you will bring some more rock on your head. I'm shut up and can't get out."

"Are you hurt?

"No."

"Wait a little longer and we'll fetch more help. We can't shift these stones alone."

"Stay with me, uncle!" I cried despairingly. "It's so horrible alone in this place."

"I'll stop here," replied my uncle reassuringly, and I heard the footsteps of the men as they went off to procure help.

"Have you a light?" asked my uncle.

"Yes—have you?"

"No—we had only one box of matches between us; but never mind, it's only a question of an hour or so."

"How long have I been here?"

"Less than an hour."

Less than an hour! It seemed six times that length of time. However, I had a kind of empty satisfaction in knowing that Uncle Herbert was in the darkness, while I, although penned in, had the benefit of a feeble light.

Notwithstanding that my uncle kept up a desultory conversation, the time passed very slowly; but before the rescue party returned I learnt that the explosives had been safely transported to the reef, and that, on my failing to return, the boat's crew had explored the cave, finding the clue of seaming-twine and following it till it disappeared between the debris. I then told him of my adventure, relating the cause of the roof caving-in, and cautioning him to prevent the others making too much noise.

At length the rescuers arrived, and, without delay, they attacked the rocks with crowbars, trying to dislodge and remove the huge boulders. For a long time they worked incessantly and energetically, but finally they desisted, and I could hear a consultation taking place, though the words were inaudible.

"I've sent for some blasting powder, Reggie," said my father. "The rocks are too large and too tightly wedged together to shift otherwise."

"Won't the explosion bring down more of the roof?" I cried out in my anxiety.

"We must take the chance. Wait a little longer and I'll tell you what to do."

There was a lull in the conversation, and I heard a dull, grinding sound, as if some steel instrument was being bored into the rock. Then, after a considerable time, my father spoke again.

"How far does the cave extend?"

"A long way, with passages on each side."

"Very well. Go about a hundred yards from this heap of rock and hide in one of the side-tunnels. Take your coat off, and place it over your head to deaden the sound. I am going to set fire to the fuse, and the explosion will take place in five minutes."

I immediately set off to a place of safety, and walking as rapidly as I could by the dim light of the candle, the floor, fortunately, being even, I counted a hundred and twenty paces; then, turning abruptly to the right, I set the candle on the ground, wrapped my head in my coat, and waited.

Presently came the short sharp crack of the explosion and a dull rumble of falling stones. A sudden rush of air, an appalling echo, and the noise of a shower of rock falling from the roof, instantly followed the detonation, and an acrid smell filled the cave.

Tearing away my coat from my head, I found that the air current had extinguished the candle, and with considerable haste I struck a match. Stones still fell at intervals from the roof, but my range of vision was limited by the feeble glimmer of the light and the thick haze of the smoke and dust caused by the explosion.

Then I heard the sound of returning footsteps, and my name was called. Hastening back to the barrier that held me captive, I saw a shaft of light from the men's lanterns glancing through a narrow hole close to the roof. The aperture was less than eighteen inches in height and slightly more in width, while its upper portion was overhung by a sharp wedge-shaped piece of rock, that reminded me forcibly of the knife of a guillotine.

"Tell him to hurry up, sir," I heard the bos'n exclaim anxiously. "A fall may take place at any moment."

"Reggie," exclaimed my father, "climb up and squeeze through that hole."

"But I can't, father!" I replied, regarding the opening with dismay.

"You must!" he repeated sternly—even harshly, it seemed. "Get up, instantly!"

Carefully I negotiated the ascent of a bank of shattered rock, till I was on a level with the hole, and, looking through, I could see the heads and shoulders of the rescue party on the other side of the barrier. But the sight of that fearful-looking piece of jagged rock overhanging the way to safety caused my courage to ebb, for in my imagination I saw it slowly, yet surely, descending to crush the life out of my body.

"Now, then, hurry up!" repeated my father, in a voice that was sterner than before.

With a despairing effort I tried to creep through the aperture, but, being unable to use my arms or legs, the attempt was useless.

"Look here, Mr. Reginald," exclaimed the bos'n, "we are going to pass a rope through to you. Put both your feet in the bowline, grip the rope like grim death with your right hand as high above your head as you can reach, and keep your left down close to your side. Give the word when you are ready, and we'll haul you through in a jiffy."

The rope was thrust through the hole by means of a long pole, and I did as I was directed, although, I am afraid, I gave the word to haul away in a very undecided tone. A steady strain on the rope, and I began to slide towards the narrow path that led to safety. Grazed by the sharp edges of the jagged rock, my knuckles, hips, and knees bleeding, and my feet jammed together by the strain on the bow-line, I felt that the perilous journey would never end.

With wide-open eyes I stared blankly at the rock above me, at one time less than six inches from my face. The confinement of the narrow passage produced a feeling of suffocation, and with it the impression that the walls of the tunnel were contracting; but at length willing hands seized my outstretched arm, then my shoulders, and I was free.

"Back, all of you!" shouted the bos'n, and in the rush for safety I was boldly carried off by one of the sailors. There was another rumbling sound, and the place through which I had just emerged was choked by a still greater fall of rock. I—nay, the whole party—had escaped by the very skin of our teeth.

No time was lost in gaining the open air. It was night, but by the glimmer of the lanterns I saw that my father's eyes were filled with tears as he kissed me—even in front of all the men.

As we were rowed back to the "Fortuna," and I sat in the stern-sheets with my father and uncle, I whispered, "What made you speak so crossly to me, pater?"

"Necessity, my boy—stern necessity. Had I not compelled you to do what I told you, your hesitation would doubtless have proved fatal, though, believe me, Reggie, you will never be able to realize your father's agony of mind when he spoke thus."

Chapter XX

A GREAT CATASTROPHE

THE next few days were spent in making final preparations for the "Fortuna's" passage to the open sea. By the removal of her ballast, and partial emptying of the water-tanks, her draught was reduced to 8 feet 6 inches.

Fenders and some stout trunks of palm-trees were lashed alongside and underneath her bilges to prevent damage in the event of the yacht touching bottom, and hawsers were prepared to warp her through the narrow opening in the reef.

Meanwhile a party of men under Uncle Herbert's directions had bored and prepared a chamber in the rock to receive nearly the whole of the remaining blasting powder, a small quantity being retained to form a "necklace"—to use the professional term—to assist in the complete dismemberment of the rock.

The work of placing the charge into the receptacle was performed by my uncle, as he preferred to take the risk alone. At dead low water springs the lagoon still remaining tidal, he took the gig, with its dangerous freight, and rowed close to the low cliff that formed the barrier between the lagoon and the open sea. Working quickly, yet cautiously, he transferred the blasting powder to the chamber, and placed a double necklace in two parallel lines in grooves over the tongue of rock. The charge was to be fired by means of a time fuse, the length of the period between the lighting of the fuse and the explosion being timed at twenty minutes. A quarter of a mile off lay the whaler, well equipped with sounding lines and rods to take the depths of the newly formed channel, and the crew anxiously awaited the appearance of the gig.

Three hours after low water the fuse was lit, and my uncle rowed back to the whaler. All eyes were fixed on the spot where the explosion was to take place, and every one who possessed a watch consulted it with feverish attention.

The twenty minutes passed, yet no explosion occurred. Five more minutes, and still no result. We began to get anxious, and my father and his brother exchanged grave looks. At the expiration of half an hour they came to the conclusion that the fuse, by some means or the other, had been extinguished, and Uncle Herbert proposed to row back and find out the cause.

"No, no," replied my father. "Give it an hour at the very least," and reluctantly my uncle agreed to defer his visit to the scene of his failure.

Directly the hour was up he rowed towards the little channel, taking two more fuses with him, but hardly had he completed half the distance when a column of smoke and dust rose into the air, followed by a deep roar. Masses of rock flew in all directions, some falling close to the gig.

"Give way, lads!" shouted the bos'n excitedly, and, bending to their oars with a will, the men urged the whaler through the water at a great pace, the heavy boat overtaking the gig before Uncle Herbert had reached the opening of the little creek, much to his chagrin.

At the head of this creek, where formerly the tongue of hard rock had been, a channel twenty feet in width communicated with the sea, and already the flood tide was swirling through. With a loud cheer, the men pulled towards the gap.

"Easy now," said the bos'n; "there might still be shallow water"; and with the blades of the oars almost touching the walls of rock on either side, the whaler breasted the tide and gained the deep water beyond.

Here we anchored, and, paying out a long grass warp, the boat was allowed to drift back into the channel, where, by careful soundings, a depth of not less than one fathom was found throughout its entire length. The action of the explosive had not only blown away the rock, but had excavated a trench with an almost even bottom.

"Two hours more to slack water," said the bos'n, consulting his watch. "We shan't get her out this tide, sir. Do you propose to try tonight?"

"No, I prefer to see what we are up to, unless it is absolutely necessary. How long will it be before the springs begin to slacken, do you think?"

"Two days at the most, sir."

"Very well; we'll make an attempt to-morrow."

Shortly after low water on the following day, the "Fortuna" weighed anchor, and with a man at the masthead to look out for shoals, and the motor softly humming, she forged slowly ahead through the calm waters of the lagoon, rolling sluggishly with the lessened draught.

On approaching the gully, two warps were laid out from the bows, one on either side, and held ashore by a party of men, and, the motor having stopped running, the yacht was slowly and carefully warped into the natural channel. Directly she was safely inside, two more warps were led from her quarters, so that those on shore had her in perfect control, only the bos'n and four seamen remaining on board.

At a snail's pace the "Fortuna" was headed for the cut that had recently been blasted, and here the yacht was made fast to await high water.

The flood now made slowly through the cutting, but, held securely by the warps, the "Fortuna" breasted the current without yawing in the eddies that swirled on either side, while my father, giving frequent glances to a rough tide-gauge, awaited the critical moment in which to make the attempt.

Gradually the current slackened, till it was barely perceptible, and the signal was given to continue warping. With a cheery "Yo-ho!" all the hands ashore, including the doctor and myself, bent to their task, and the "Fortuna" started on her final bid for freedom.

Suddenly there was a slight jar, and the yacht, trembling like a live creature, brought up. With feverish anxiety, my father jumped into the gig, which had already been brought through the gap, and examined the water around the yacht's bows. A rough sounding gave him five fathoms, while aft, where she had taken ground, there was not one and a half fathoms.

"We must move her," he shouted. "If she's caught on a falling tide on the ledge, she'll break her back."

"Tide's ebbing already, sir," exclaimed the bos'n. "Send every man aboard and start the motor. 'Tis a last chance."

With the utmost haste we jumped into the boats and boarded the "Fortuna," and, leaving one man as boat-keeper, every available member of the crew, gathered on the fo'c'sle, all jumping in time to help to free the yacht from the tenacious ledge.

The motor was set running, at full speed, and the bos'n alone remained aft at the wheel.

"Altogether; shake her up!" was the cry, and we all jumped with renewed energy. There was a dull grating sound, and the "Fortuna," slipping off the rock, glided into deep water and headed with increasing speed towards the open sea.

In obedience to an order the men rushed aft, for the propeller was almost out of the water, while Mr. Wilkins had the greatest difficulty in keeping the yacht on her course; nor did she bring up till she had passed without the natural breakwaters and over the patch of deep water.

As she passed the whaler and the gig, the boat-keeper had dexterously thrown a line on board, and both boats were safely in tow of the yacht.

A sounding gave five fathoms, and the anchors were let go, and the "Fortuna" was safely moored well clear of the dangerous reef.

"There's no time to be lost, sir," said the bos'n. "We are in an exposed berth, and a gale might spring up at an hour's notice."

"That's true," replied my father. "And though the glass is steady, I prefer to take no risks. It's a pity, though, that we are so far from shore."

"It's as near as we can lie in safety, sir. There's foul ground close to the reef, and the deep water between it and the bank on which we've brought up is far too deep to anchor in. There's no bottom at a hundred fathoms.

"Another freak of nature, I suppose. However, we must make the best of things. Pipe away both boats, if you please, Mr. Wilkins, and we'll start loading up at once."

Delighted with their success, the crew worked with a will, and both boats put off for the lagoon to load up the silver pigs and money-chests, only my father, Dr. Conolly, Yadillah, and myself remaining on the yacht.

In a little over two hours' time we saw them returning through the cutting. The whaler, deeply laden with its precious cargo, was leading, the gig, also carrying some of the specie, being towed astern, with only one man to steer.

"I don't like the look of that boat," remarked the doctor, pointing to the whaler. "She's far too deep in the water."

"Oh, it's safe enough," replied my father. "The sea's calm, and, besides, Wilkins knows what he's about."

We continued watching the progress of the boats as they slowly approached the "Fortuna." They had cleared the seaward arms of the natural breakwaters, and were entering the dark-blue patch that indicated the deep water, when about a hundred or two hundred yards off a column of water flew up in the air, and amidst the descending spray a huge black shape appeared above the surface. "A whale!" exclaimed my father and the doctor simultaneously.

"I hope it won't attack the boats," added Dr. Conolly.

"I think not. I've never known or heard of a whale attacking a boat unless when struck by a harpoon."

"You haven't? Begorra!" exclaimed the doctor excitedly, bursting into a Hibernian expression for the first time during his stay on the yacht. "Then ye'll see it now."

As he spoke the whale made directly for the boats as if it recognized in the whaler the shape of an enemy.

With a furious exclamation, my father sprang towards the Q.-F., which happened to be uncovered, and, wrenching open the breech-block, thrust a cartridge into the chamber; then, placing his shoulder against the shoulder-piece, he swung the gun round towards the advancing monster, but before his finger could touch the trigger the doctor grasped his arm and forcibly dragged him away.

"We can do nothing," he muttered grimly. "See, the boats are already in the line of fire." My father, realizing that the discharge of the gun would result in the destruction of the boats in addition to the annihilation of the whale, rushed to the side and awaited the inevitable onslaught.

With great rapidity the huge monster made straight for its prey, and from the boats shouts and cries of terror arose when the men became aware of their peril. Some of the crew stood up, brandishing their oars, to offer a puny resistance to the oncoming mass of animal energy, others jumped overboard, and swam in all directions, while the bos'n, with admirable presence of mind, drew his knife and cut the painter that led from the stern of the whaler to the gig.

The next instant the whale seemed to lift its ponderous carcass clear of the water; then, diving deeply beneath the downed boat, it struck it an irresistible blow with its massive tail.

A shower of splinters and spray rose in the air, and amidst a veritable maelstrom, the whaler, with its priceless freight, disappeared beneath the waves, and the troubled water was dotted with the heads of the swimmers and a jumble of floating oars and pieces of broken wood.

The bulk of the treasure of the "San Philipo" was irrecoverably lost.

Satisfied with the mischief it had wrought, the whale had disappeared. The crew of the lost boat swam towards the gig, and several began climbing over the low sides of the deeply laden little craft.

"Why, if they are not careful, they'll sink her, too," exclaimed my father in blank despair, but, fortunately, the swimmers realised the risk, for, taking hold of the gunwales and lightly supporting themselves, they allowed the men who had already clambered on board to take the oars, and the gig made slowly for the "Fortuna."

Happening to look towards Dr. Conolly, I noticed he had his eyes fixed on the boat and was counting in an audible voice "... eight, nine, ten, eleven," and simultaneously the awful truth flashed in our minds—there was one man missing.

"Surely not!" exclaimed my father in a horrified voice. "Surely not! Count again, Conolly. Perhaps we cannot see every one. Isn't that a man's head just showing above the boat's quarter?"

"... nine, ten, eleven."

There was no mistake in the numbers. Another man had gone to his last account, and who was it? Not my uncle; he was in the water, holding on to the side of the boat; nor the bos'n, nor Lord, the quartermaster. Dailey, Stainer, and Mills were in the boat. Hinks, Money, Lewis, Burbidge, and Alec Johnston, they were safe. Then only Joe Dirham remained to be accounted for.

"Where's Dirham?" shouted my father as the boat crept alongside and was made fast.

"Gone, sir," replied the survivors in a chorus. "Dragged down by the whaler as she sank."

The men came in over the side, and the gig, with four of the boxes of specie, was hauled up in the davits, and despondently, the crew went for'ard to change their saturated garments.

For a while my father remained lost in thought, gazing blankly at the spot where the whaler had sunk, the blue now peaceful and unruffled. At length, overcome by the bitterness of his emotion, he turned on his heel and sought the solitude of his cabin.

But pressing work had to be done. The whole of the iron ballast, including the quantity which we had hoped would be supplanted by the pigs of silver, had to be replaced with the utmost dispatch; the water tanks had to be refilled, and stores procured from the island. Working day and night in relays, the crew accomplished their task within forty hours, and the "Fortuna" was ready for her long homeward voyage.

Chapter XXI

CHECKMATE

"I WANT to ask your advice upon a certain matter, Mr. Herbert," said the bos'n to my uncle that same evening. The "Fortuna" still remained at anchor, for we were unwilling, owing to the changes caused by the seismic disturbance, to make a passage in the darkness through the shoals that surrounded the island.

My uncle and I were seated in deck chairs enjoying the cool of the evening as well as our depressed spirits would allow, when Mr. Wilkins approached, holding a bundle of papers in his hand.

"Well, what is it, Mr. Wilkins?"

"I've just been overhauling poor Dirham's ditty-box, sir, and there's something queer about these letters. I thought I'd best show them to you before I mention the matter to Mr. Trevena."

"They are all from the same individual, I notice," remarked Uncle Herbert as he glanced at the address. "This, I take it, is the first."

It was a plain envelope, on which was written, "Mr. J. Dirham, Yacht 'Fortuna,' Malta." Taking out the contents, Uncle Herbert held a sheet of closely written paper up to the light of a deck lamp. On the top of the paper was the heading, *The Yachtsman's Fortnightly Journal*, with an address at Plymouth.

DEAR SIR. (it ran),—
We are in receipt of your letter of the 21st ult., and note the information given of "Fortuna" yacht as arranged. Kindly let us

know as soon as can be ascertained the lat. and long. of the island to which you go. A further sum of five shillings has been placed to your credit in our ledgers.

Yours very truly,
JAMES TICKET (Editor).

"There's something fishy about this, Mr. Wilkins. In the first place, I don't believe there is such a journal as *The Yachtsman's Fortnightly*, and, secondly, no editor would pen such un-English jargon."

"That's what I thought, sir; now read this one."

The second communication was addressed to the yacht at Point de Galle, Ceylon, and thanked the recipient for the information regarding the position of San Philipo Island. Curiously enough, it was signed "James Trickett," a difference of two letters to the signature of the previous epistle.

"Do you think we might show them to Mr. Trevena?" asked the bos'n. "I don't like to worry him, seeing him so cut up just at present.

"I don't think it will do him any harm," replied my uncle. "If anything, it will give him something to occupy his mind. I am of the opinion that some underhand business is afloat, and that Dirham was an agent in the matter. However, we'll see what my brother has to say about it."

So saying, he led the way to the cabin, where my father was sitting brooding over the calamities of the day. Without speaking, my uncle handed him the packet of letters, which my father carelessly took, but before he had read the first two or three his face lighted up with animated interest.

"What do you make of the business?" asked my uncle. "It seems a bit of a mystery?"

"A mystery? My word!—the whole affair is as clear as daylight. An interested party, or parties, must have been trying to find out the destination of the 'Fortuna' in order to try, and cut her out, as it were. What surprises me is that a rival expedition has not appeared on the scene before now; but let them come," he added bitterly; "they are welcome to what's left."

"Then you think the *Yachtsman's Fortnightly Journal* is a myth!"

"Undoubtedly. There never was such a periodical, and it is merely a blind. Dirham was a traitor, though perhaps he acted in ignorance of the jeopardy, in which he might have placed us, thinking that he was merely giving commonplace information to a yachting paper; and I am convinced that, judging by the orthographical and grammatical errors in these letters, the author is none other than your Brazilian friend, the fellow you shot when he broke into our house."

"Your explanation seems plausible."

"Nothing could be more simple. The Brazilian received the particulars of the position of the island from Dirham, who, judging by the postmarks and addresses on these envelopes, sent the information from Port Said or Suez. It was after we left Malta, you remember, that the latitude and longitude of the island became an open secret. No doubt the villain, who may be a man of wealth or at least of considerable means, knew far more about the treasure than we are aware. He might have wormed part of the secret from Ross Trevena or his son during their residence near Pernambuco. However, he receives the information, for, as you see here, he acknowledges the receipt of it, and I'll be greatly surprised if a private steam-yacht has not been chartered to try and carry off the treasure before we arrived at the island."

"I should like to witness their disappointment," remarked my uncle.

"It would not be greater than mine is," replied my father, relapsing into a depressed tone at the thought of our ill-fortune. "Two poor fellows have been sacrificed to the lust of gold, and the bulk of the treasure lies at the bottom of the sea."

"You may recover it yet, 'sir," exclaimed the bos'n. "The divers are willing to make the attempt, and it may be that there is less water at the spot where the whaler sank than we know of."

"No, Mr. Wilkins," replied my father emphatically, "I'll have no more lives risked in the matter. The stuff can stay where it is. After all, we have not done so badly, if we do not take into consideration the two deplorable fatalities. The two large chests, four boxes of specie, and the gold plate are not to be sneezed at, and, as I have already announced to the crew, every man will be well provided for when the treasure is shared out. Even now we have done better than most of the treasure-hunting syndicates that have been formed in recent years, for we have a substantial balance in hand."

"Then we'll weigh anchor to-morrow, sir?" asked the bos'n. "Everything is shipshape—stores, water, and ballast are aboard."

"You must have worked well," exclaimed my father enthusiastically. "Yes, to-morrow at daybreak."

* * * * *

The rasping of the windlass and the clinking of the cable as it came slowly inboard were the welcome sounds that greeted my ears early the next morning, and, jumping out of my bunk, I proceeded to dress in order to have a glimpse of San Philipo Island before it was lost to view. But before I was half-way through that operation a hoarse voice shouted "Sail-ho!"

"What can that be?" I asked myself.

The next instant the bos'n came running down the companion, and, knocking at the door of my father's cabin, he exclaimed—

"A large steam-yacht approaching, sir!"

"Any flag?"

"No, sir; she shows no colours."

"How far away is she?"

"About two miles to the south-east, and she's making straight for the island."

"The rival treasure-seekers!" I exclaimed excitedly. "Now for some excitement," and, hastily completing my toilet, I rushed on deck, where Uncle Herbert, Dr. Conolly, and the crew, save those who manned the windlass, were intently watching the approach of the strange craft. Presently we were joined by my father.

The vessel, which had apparently been making about eleven knots, was now within half a mile, and her engines were eased down preparatory to anchoring. She was about two hundred tons displacement, with schooner bows, and carried two pole masts. With a telescope I saw the crew, clustered up for'ard, regarding us with the same curiosity that we were bestowing upon them. They were mostly dark-featured, some being black, and were rigged out in white canvas clothing and red-stocking caps. On the bridge were five or six men, evidently officers, in dark-blue uniforms; plentifully embellished with gold lace and buttons. A more inappropriate uniform for the tropics would be hard to obtain, unless it were a motor-coat; but it seemed evident from their love of finery; that these men came from a Latin nation—Italy or Spain, or one of their offshoots.

"Up and down!" shouted the bos'n, who was superintending the weighing of the anchor, referring to the fact that the chain had already taken the weight of our ground-tackle off the bottom'.

"Avast heaving!" he continued, at a sign from my father, and the clanking of the winch ceased, the dripping anchor hanging just clear of the surface. In the tideless sea, with not a breath of wind to ruffle the absolutely calm water, the "Fortuna" lay motionless, awaiting the approach of her rival.

"Blest if I don't know 'er!" exclaimed one of the crew. "Why, if she ain't the old 'Ermyhony' that used ter lie off Priddy's. 'Ard when I was in the 'Nelson' I'll eat my 'at."

"The what did he say?" I asked the doctor.

"The 'Hermione' I suppose he means," he replied with a smile.

"Hoist our colours," ordered my father, and the blue ensign was run up to the mizzen-truck, where it hung motionless in the still atmosphere.

The strange yacht still held on her course, and slowly, so slowly that it seemed like an exhibition of sulky reluctance, her ensign was hoisted, and simultaneously, with a heavy splash and a loud rattle of chain, the anchor was let go.

To me, her colours, as they hung in folds from her mainmast head, appeared to be a mixture of blue, green, and yellow, but my ignorance of their nationality was dispelled by a general exclamation, "The Brazilian ensign!"

"There you are! Am I not right?" said my father.

"Yes," replied Uncle Herbert, who was studying the group on the bridge through a glass. "And see that fellow by the chart-house door, the second from the end? I would know him anywhere in spite of his brass-bound togs. It's our old acquaintance, *alias* James Ticket, right enough. But see him scowl!"

"They're signalling, sir," said Lord, the quartermaster, as a string, of bunting fluttered up from her bridge.

"International code: 'I want to communicate,'" reported the bos'n.

"Reply in the negative," repeated my father; "and give my compliments to the Editor of the *Yachtsman's Fortnightly.*"

The motor throbbed, and the "Fortuna," gathering way, showed her stern to the Brazilian yacht, the crew of which were dividing their attention between the vessel that had baulked their enterprise and the gaunt outlines of the hulk of the "San Philipo," as, raised on the summit of the reef, she stood out boldly against the cliffs of the treasure island.

In another hour we had caught a favouring breeze, and the scene of our many and varied adventures had disappeared beneath the horizon. The "Fortuna" was homeward bound.

* * * * *

Little remains to be said concerning the "San Philipo" treasure. The "Fortuna" had a long, though pleasant, passage home, Dr. Conolly leaving the yacht at Singapore, where he received a cablegram from London offering him his long-desired post as medical officer on a liner.

Yadillah took his discharge at Suez, and, with a fair share of the spoils, announced his intention of setting up as a bumboatman at that port.

Eighteen months after our departure the "Fortuna" entered Fowey Harbour, where an enthusiastic welcome awaited us.

Once more we were back in our home at Polruan, Alec Johnston remaining as a trusted servant. The rest of the crew of the "Fortuna" have scattered far and wide, but we frequently hear from most of them, while the bos'n and the quartermaster, who have bought pretty little cottages near Falmouth, often pay us a welcome visit.

The proceeds of the residue of the treasure have been judiciously invested, and the only thing that apparently troubles my father is the importunities of the Inland Revenue authorities.

One link serves to remind me forcibly of the past. Over the door of the now rebuilt summer-house that had played an important part in this story is fixed the huge graven image which we had brought from the treasure island; and I never look at it without vividly recalling the terrifying ordeal I underwent when lying bound and helpless before the figure-head of the "San Philipo."

www.ingramcontent.com/pod-product-compliance
Lightning Source LLC
Chambersburg PA
CBHW061211210726
48294CB00006B/1809